COWBOY CLASSIFIEDS

Cowboy
seeking a
SECOND
CHANCE

JANICE WHITEAKER

CHAPTER ONE

"WHAT'S GOING ON here?"

Boone stood just inside the back door of the house where he grew up, staring at the scene in front of him.

His mother sat at the long kitchen table with two other women. One he didn't know.

One he did.

Mae Wells sat at his mother's side, wearing a smile that was too tight to be genuine.

The sight of her should probably scare the hell out of him considering the last time he saw her she pointed a chef's knife at the center of his chest.

But seeing Mae in this house brought on a feeling that was so much worse than fear.

Regret.

"Mae has agreed to help me find the general manager for The Inn." His mother matched Mae's smile. "Isn't that sweet of her?"

Sweet was not a word he'd use to describe the woman in front of him.

Not anymore.

And the fact intrigued him more than it should.

"Awful sweet of her." Boone got his boots moving in the direction he'd been headed. He tipped his head at the line of women as he passed. "If you'll excuse me."

He could feel Mae's eyes on him as he walked toward the hall leading to the front of the large farmhouse. No doubt she was shooting daggers into his back. Daggers his mother most certainly believed he deserved.

She wasn't wrong.

Boone hustled up the stairs, ready to get out of the house for more reasons than one. He grabbed a fresh pair of jeans from Wyatt's closet before hurrying back down to the main floor. He eyed the front door, considering the convenient escape option.

But he wasn't a coward.

Idle chat fell to silence as he entered the kitchen, all three women watching as he walked to the back door. He offered a smile. "Enjoy the rest of your afternoon."

He didn't wait for a response. There wouldn't be one.

Which was fine.

By the time Boone made it to the barn Brody already had Wyatt out of his cow patty-covered jeans. He passed the fresh pants to his soon-to-be-official nephew. "You all owe me one. I coulda died getting those for you."

"How's that?" Brody helped Wyatt balance as the kid wiggled into the clean jeans.

"Mae's in there with Mom and some other woman." Boone bent to line Wyatt's boots up so they'd be easy to pull on. "Luckily there were no weapons within reach."

"I'm not sure that would stop her." Brody crouched down

to pull Wyatt's jeans over his boots. He glanced up at the son he'd already claimed as his own. "Feel better, Little Man?"

Wyatt's head bobbed in a nod. "A lot."

"You smell better too." Brody mussed Wyatt's dark hair. "Ready to get back out there?"

"Yup. I'll be careful getting off Abigail this time." Wyatt tucked his shirt into his jeans as he and Brody walked toward the front of the barn where their horses were tied up.

"It happens." Brody stood by as Wyatt mounted up, making sure the boy was situated before climbing onto his own horse. He grinned Boone's way. "You aren't the first man around here to find himself in a pile of sh—" his gaze went to the boy at his side, "crap."

Wyatt was still giggling as they headed back out, leaving Boone standing alone in the yard, watching the father and son as they rode away.

Brody's language wasn't the only thing about him that had changed recently. Since his future wife's arrival at the ranch, Brody was happier and more relaxed than he'd been in years. Originally, Clara moved to the ranch with her son Wyatt to work as the nanny for Brody's twin daughters, but she'd ended up being so much more. They both had.

And now Boone got to watch their damn fairy tale from sunup to sundown.

"You gonna just stand there or are you gonna actually help me?" His youngest brother Brett stood at the open barn door, a hay bale in his hands.

Boone gave the house a sidelong glance as he turned. "I'm comin'."

He'd been gone for almost ten years and the hierarchy in the family had most definitely changed.

And now he was at the bottom.

That meant when stalls had to be stripped he was the man for the job.

He spent the rest of the afternoon clearing out soiled straw and laying fresh. Scrubbing feed buckets and water troughs, clearing away the ick that built up in the warming spring weather.

By the time the barn was clean and fresh he was anything but, covered in filth and sweat and stinking to high heaven.

His body ached and his skin itched, but the manual labor was a welcome distraction. One he relied on day in and day out.

Boone took off his hat as he walked out of the barn, using a handkerchief to wipe the sweat from his brow before putting each back in place. Brett rounded the barn with the final bale of hay to be dished out. They cut the ties and finished splitting it between the last two stalls just as the sound of voices carried into the barn from outside. Boone went to the open sliding door expecting to see his other two brothers coming back from the fields with their father and Wyatt.

But it turned out the voices he'd barely heard over the drone of the fans in the barn weren't male.

"Who is that?" Brett stood staring in the same direction.

"Don't know." The other woman he'd seen with his mother and Mae was pretty enough. She had long, light brown hair and a curvy frame that probably caught the eye of most men.

Except when she stood next to someone like Mae.

Mae was something special. Always had been. It's why

she was his the minute he knew enough to convince her to be.

It was also why he deserved to muck stalls every day for the rest of his life.

Because ten years ago he was stupid enough to convince himself there was something better out there.

Not woman wise.

Life wise.

"I'll be back." Boone stepped toward where Mae and the other woman were walking toward their cars.

Brett laughed, leaning back against the barn. "Where you wanna be buried?"

"Shut up." Boone kept walking.

He knew better than this. Mae wanted to stab him the last time they ran into each other. He saw it in her eyes.

And he would have let her. Maybe then she'd hate him less.

Boone caught up to them. "You find someone?"

The women turned his way, each set of eyes carrying a similar level of disdain.

Clearly Mae made sure her new friend understood what a piece of shit he was.

Boone wiped one palm down the side of his jeans before holding it out to the unidentified woman. "I'm Boone."

The woman's gaze dropped to his hand before sliding Mae's way. She took the offer, shaking with a grip tight enough to solidify his suspicions. "Nora."

"Are you the new cook?" Boone tried to look relaxed, but the way Mae's eyes moved over him made him anything but.

Nora snorted. "Not a chance." She backed away. "I'll see you later, Mae."

Mae's grey eyes went wide as Nora abandoned her, the other woman ducking into her car with a wave and a smile before pulling away.

"Not much of a friend, is she?"

Mae's gaze snapped his way, eyes immediately narrowing. "What's that supposed to mean?"

"Means she just ditched you with the man who broke your heart."

Mae's lips lifted at the edges in an unseen smile. "My heart's not broken, Boone." She lifted a brow. "It's perfectly fine and tended to."

"Tended to?" It was an unfair thing, his reaction. He was the one who fucked up. He was the one who left, walked away from something that was more than an nineteen-year-old kid ever could have realized.

But the thought of another man tending to Mae made his insides burn.

Not that he'd ever tended to her as a man. It was one of many great regrets he had in his life.

"You heard me." Mae stood tall in front of him, back straight, chin high in the air. Not a trace of the girl he once knew peeking through the steel front she showed him.

That was his fault too.

"I don't know what you thought happened when you left here, Boone Pace, but if you expected me to be sitting at home waiting for you to come back then you're dead wrong." Her eyes skimmed down him, appraising in a way he might have appreciated under other circumstances. "You aren't the only one who moved on."

"If you moved on I would have known about it." It was the thing that settled him the most when he first came home. Knowing that no one else had done what he hadn't been able to as a nineteen-year-old dumbass.

"You think?" Mae snorted. "I'm not the only one you left here, Boone." Her gaze was cool as it held his. "If you think their loyalty still sits with you then you get to be dead wrong twice." She turned away, heading for the shiny new SUV sitting next to his truck.

He should let her go. Let her walk away from him the same way he walked away from her.

But he was never good at doing what he should.

It's what landed him here in the first place.

Boone went after her, his boots crunching across the gravel drive. "What's his name then?"

He wanted to hear that he was right. That Mae wasn't going home to a man infinitely smarter than he was.

He wanted to hear that he wasn't the only one who never seemed able to move on. Never seemed able to forget what they had.

"His name is none of your business." Mae didn't slow down and she sure as hell didn't look his way. "No part of my life is any of your business anymore."

Boone raced her to the side of her vehicle, rushing to open her door, the manners his mother ingrained in him only half the reason.

Mae shoved her hand against the door, slamming it shut just as he opened it. Her glare was unwavering as she faced him down. "Go away, Boone. I don't need you, or any other man, treating me like I can't do for myself."

That was an interesting statement. One that cooled the selfish burn of jealousy biting at his skin. "That's good to know." He leaned a little closer, her words relaxing him more with each passing second. "Wouldn't want a man treating you like he planned to take care of you."

Mae yanked the door to her car open and tossed her bag across the front. It bounced off the passenger's door before landing in the seat, face down, contents spilling out.

But Mae didn't seem to notice. Her eyes were fixed on him.

And for one blessed second he saw the girl he remembered. The girl who stole his heart and hid it so well he didn't realize she had it until it was too late.

But then she was gone, replaced by a woman he wanted to know better in spite of the fact that what *she* wanted was for him to be in a hole somewhere.

"Expecting someone to take care of you is the biggest mistake any woman can make." Her eyes snapped down the front of him, one side of her nose lifting in response. "Go take a shower. You stink." She slammed her door, scowling at him as she backed out from her spot and turned down the main drive.

That could have gone better.

Could've gone a hell of a lot worse too. He didn't have a ten-inch blade between his ribs, and when Mae was involved that could be counted as a win.

"She's right." Brett was still in the same spot as Boone walked past.

"About?" Boone strode into the barn, Brett hot on his heels.

"You do stink." Brett stuck right with him, following a little too close.

"You got more to say?" Boone dodged Edgar's head as the

horse stuck it over the gate, looking for affection. He reached up to rub across the gelding's cheek.

"Nope." Brett lifted one shoulder. "I don't need to tell you what Mom'll do to you if you try to chase Mae again."

"Who said I was gonna try?" Boone leaned again as Edgar tried to bump him with his head.

"You'd be stupid not to." Brett grinned. "Almost as stupid as you'd have to be to try."

"Mae hates my guts." He stroked down Edgar's neck, working up the will to haul his stinking ass to the cabin where he spent his nights.

Alone.

"There's a thin line between love and hate, Brother." Brett winked. "Course if you're on the wrong end of it you might end up worse off than you are now."

"Now? What's wrong with how I am now?" Boone gave Edgar a final pet before stepping away from his stall to avoid getting roped into standing there forever.

"Not a single woman's been to that cabin since you moved back."

"So?"

"So? You've been gone so long you're fresh damn meat here. You could have a different girl in your bed every night." Brett's tone carried a hint of jealousy. "The rest of us are all old fuckin' news. The least you could do is take advantage of it."

He didn't want to take advantage of it. He'd had his share of women. His share of one-night-stands.

They weren't all they were cracked up to be. They all ended the same way.

Alone.

But thinking it and saying it were two different things. "Who says I'm not in their beds?"

Brett had the balls to laugh. "Your ass is in that cabin every night when the sun goes down. If you're in and out of their beds before that then they should kick your minuteman ass out."

The bell at the house started to ring, loud and clear.

"Shit." Boone glanced down at his filth-covered shirt and jeans. His mother would kill him for coming to dinner like he was. "I'm heading out." He'd rather deal with finding his own food than his mother's wrath.

And she was most definitely going to be worked up after having the reminder of everything he'd done wrong staring at her all afternoon.

"Probably best." Brett tipped his head toward the house. "Want me to bring you anything as I come in?"

Brett and Brooks, his younger brothers, shared a large cabin out near the row of smaller cabins reserved for hands and sons who ruined their mother's lives.

"I'll be fine." Boone fished the keys to his truck out of his pocket. "See you in the morning." He climbed into the cab, the enclosed space making just how bad he smelled even clearer than before.

Chasing Mae down like this probably wasn't his best move.

Boone drove to the cabin he'd been living in since coming back from nearly a decade traveling the country as a rodeo cowboy, living out his dream.

What he tried to convince himself was his dream.

At first he was right. He loved the excitement. The notoriety. Getting to see places he'd never dreamed of.

But now that he was on the other end of it, everything looked a hell of a lot different.

He parked the truck and bailed out, ready to get cleaned up and call it a day. The cabin was silent as he went in, peeling off the layers of sweat-soaked clothing on his way toward the bathroom at the back of the small space. A hot shower and thorough scrub made him feel human again.

But it didn't come close to touching the unrest that tainted every inch of his life.

Boone pulled on a fresh t-shirt and a pair of athletic pants before sitting on the edge of his single bed to tie on his running shoes. Skipping dinner sounded fine when all he could smell was his own stink, but now that he was clean his stomach was protesting that option.

Any other night he'd go raid the fridge at the main house, but the last thing he wanted right now was to listen to his mother remind him of everything he already knew.

He snagged his keys off the small table tucked into the front corner and headed out into the warm spring air. The sun was setting behind heavy-looking clouds as most of the hands filtered into their cabins, worn out from another long day.

He was right there with them, only his exhaustion wasn't just from today.

And it was nothing a good-night's sleep could ever fix.

CHAPTER TWO

"WAS HE THERE?"

"Of course he was there." Mae dropped her bag onto the counter in the kitchen of The Wooden Spoon. She leaned against the edge beside it, eyeing the woman puttering around the space. "Why are you still here?"

Camille wouldn't meet her gaze. "There was just a lot left to do."

"You're only on the schedule until four." She'd hired Camille almost six months ago, even though technically she didn't need another set of hands.

And didn't really have the funds to pay for them. Every bit of extra went to paying off the loan she took out to open the restaurant.

But Camille needed the income and the possible freedom it could give her.

Camille's head tipped her way. "I already clocked out. I don't expect you to pay me for this."

"I don't feel right not paying you for the work you do, Camille." Mae pulled out the stool tucked under the counter and dropped onto it. "But don't you have a kid at home waiting for you?"

Camille's eyes drifted back to the assembly line she was scrubbing within an inch of its life. "He's staying with my momma tonight."

"Oh." Mae's stomach turned a little.

"I just thought I'd get a little ahead here since Calvin isn't home anyway." Camille gave her a tight smile. "That's all."

Mae dug deep to find a smile of her own. One that was nearly impossible to wear. "That's a good idea then."

Camille glanced at the clock on the wall. "Don't you have a date?"

"I do." Mae pushed up from her seat with a sigh.

Camille seemed to relax a little at the change of conversation. Her shoulders dropped down as she swiped across the stainless-steel surface she'd already wiped ten times. "I thought you were excited about this guy?"

She was.

But that was before Boone came along and pissed all over her good mood. "I am." Mae tried to pull up the anticipation she'd felt this morning about the date, but it just wouldn't come.

Camille scanned her from head to toe. "Better go get ready then."

"You saying I shouldn't go like this?" She grinned a little, turning from side to side. She was still in the fitted jeans and logoed t-shirt she wore every day to work.

Camille laughed. A sound Mae hardly heard from her friend anymore. "I mean if you set the bar low from the beginning it might work in your favor."

Mae picked up a towel from the counter and tossed it at

Camille. "Whatever." She grabbed her purse. "I guess I'll go try to lift the bar a little." Mae turned toward the back staircase that led to the second and third floors of the old building she bought five years ago. "Lock up when you're done."

"I will." Camille leaned to peek at her. "Have fun tonight. I hope he's as hot as he looks."

"I'd say the chances of that are slim to none." Mae hustled up the stairs, unlocking the door leading to the home she'd made for herself.

It was nothing like the farmhouse she'd imagined as a younger girl.

And maybe it was better that way.

Mae tossed her purse onto the couch as she walked through the living room. "Freaking Boone."

The man always knew just how to ruin her day.

By breathing.

And of course today he had to do it all sweaty and dirty, the cling of his shirt reminding her that Boone was nothing like the boy who broke her heart all those years ago.

At least not on the outside.

Now he was all man. Tall and broad and filled out in all the right places.

Too bad he didn't get fat and bald like half the guys they went to school with.

Including the man Camille was avoiding going home to.

Mae stripped off her work clothes, dumping them straight into the washing machine and closing the door. Nothing was worse than a house that smelled like fried food and garlic.

Except maybe a house that smelled like filthy cowboy.

She took a quick shower, scrubbing all the important parts, before slicking on a layer of scented lotion. After drying her hair Mae threw in some curls with an iron. Wearing her long hair down wasn't usually an option, so she wanted to take full advantage of the opportunity. A quick make-up job later she was in front of her closet staring down the limited choices.

She pulled on a dress that spent most of its time on a hanger and slid her feet into a pair of wedge sandals, tugging the ankle strap over her heel as she hopped toward the door, trying not to break her neck.

That would be an unfortunate end to an already crappy day.

Her steps were loud as she raced down the stairs. The lights were off on the main floor and there was no sign of Camille.

She'd text her later. Make sure her friend was okay. Hopefully Camille's asshole of a husband was already passed out when she got home.

Mae locked the back door behind her and went straight to her SUV, fighting with the fabric of her dress as she fell into the driver's seat.

Her belt snapped to a stop as she yanked it out hard enough to activate the safety mechanism.

Mae let it go and closed her eyes, taking a deep breath.

She needed to calm down. Put Boone out of her mind.

Which is exactly where he belonged. He didn't own any real estate there. Not anymore.

She'd bought it all back.

Mae let out the breath and put on a smile as she started the engine.

She was going on a date with a hopefully-attractive sales manager at a polymer company. It was going to be great.

Just great.

The drive to Billings was almost forty-five minutes.

Plenty of time for it to start raining.

But that was fine. She had an umbrella in the backseat.

This date was still going to be great.

Just great.

Mae pulled into the restaurant a minute early.

She flailed around a little, twisting in her seat as she grabbed at the back floorboards looking for the umbrella. Her fingers barely tipped against the handle, forcing her to fight her way onto her knees to reach the damn thing. Her dress tangled around her body as Mae wiggled back forward facing. She took a deep breath, calming the frustration lingering from—

No. There was no frustration from anything. She was freaking peachy.

The rain started to come down harder, pelting the hood of her SUV in drops so big they seemed to bounce off the shimmery green surface.

Mae snagged her purse and shoved open the door, stepping out into the pouring rain.

And right into a puddle that was at least three inches deep.

"Fuuuuu—" Her eyes caught with the wide gaze of the little boy in the car idling the next space over.

Mae clamped her lips together, lifting them into what hopefully looked like a smile.

Her shoes would dry. They would have plenty of time

while she was sitting inside, eating a lovely dinner and drinking a glass of wine.

Maybe two.

She managed to dodge two more mini lakes in the lot on her way to the door of the restaurant, keeping the number of wet feet she had to one.

A little old man held the door for her as she hurried under the overhang. He smiled, his wrinkled face warm and kind.

It made the smile she's struggled to find all day easier to wear. "Thank you."

He tipped his head her way. "You have a good night."

Mae paused. "I will."

She was done letting Boone Pace's reappearance ruin the happiness she'd worked so hard to find.

To build.

Mae shook out the soaked umbrella, knocking as much water loose as she could before tying it up and heading to the hostess station. She found another easy smile. "Hi. I'm meeting someone."

The young woman glanced at the list in front of her. "They must not be here yet. We don't have anyone expecting an arrival."

Mae glanced around, eyeing the bar in case the man she'd been talking to for nearly three weeks decided to wait for her there.

"You can check the bar if you want." The girl gave her a sympathetic smile. "Maybe they're over there."

Mae eyed the skinny blonde who couldn't be more than eighteen.

She'd been there. Young and pretty and full of hope.

Thinking she'd never be getting stood up for a first date.

Thinking she'd never have a first date.

"Thanks." Mae's smile was gone as she wove through the people milling around the waiting area and into the bar. She scanned the male heads lined down the high-counter, looking for one that matched the man who'd sent her a handful of pictures and called her at least a dozen times.

It had to be at least ten after by now. Maybe he was caught in traffic.

Helping an old lady across the street.

In the pouring rain.

Mae slowly worked her way back to the waiting area where couples and families lined the benches, flashing pagers in hand.

"Scoot down and give the lady room to sit, honey." A mother about her age reached for the little boy sprawled across the bench they occupied. She hefted him up and onto her lap, scrunching her face up at Mae. "Sorry."

"Don't be." Mae eased down onto the spot out of obligation. "Thank you." She watched as the mother snuggled the little boy, listening to his small voice talk about something he clearly found extremely interesting. The man with them smiled as he reached out to tickle the wiggly little boy.

Mae dropped her eyes to her purse, forcing her focus away from something that would easily drag her down to a place she'd worked so hard to fight her way out of. The past was done.

The future was what she chose to make it.

And she was choosing to be happy.

The vibration of her purse made her jump. For a second

she thought it was the pager, alerting that her table was ready.

Except she didn't have a pager.

Mae dug into her bag, the illumination from her phone identifying it as the source of the buzzing. She swiped across the screen, accessing the incoming message.

The first line of the text stole what little good mood she had left.

I'm sorry.

The rest went on to explain that while she was smart and funny and attractive, Mae just wasn't what he was looking for.

Apparently he wanted stupid, boring, and ugly then.

But wait. Another text came through.

Nope. What he wanted was someone 'less consumed by their career'.

Did anyone ever say that to a man?

Probably not.

Mae stood up, the sole of her left foot squishing against the soaked lining of her shoe.

She gave the hostess a tight smile as she marched past and straight out the door.

And back into the rain.

She snapped the umbrella open and ran into the lot. Now the water was unavoidable. The downpour flooded the entirety of the blacktop. Water splashed up and onto her dress, soaking her from the knees down as she ran. Mae practically leapt into her car, tossing the dripping umbrella across the seat into the passenger's floorboard as she yanked her door closed.

On her fucking dress.

Opening it a crack she yanked at the fabric, trying to get it free without getting even more wet.

Rip.

Mother—

Mae dropped her head to the headrest, gripping the wheel as she fought between screaming at the top of her lungs.

Or crying.

But she'd cried enough.

It wasn't who she was. Not anymore.

She wasn't the woman who cried over a man. There were plenty to go around.

You could practically find them on the side of the road.

Mae carefully opened the door once more, gently pulling her torn dress free before closing it again. She glanced in the rear view mirror, catching her reflection.

At least her hair still looked good.

She eyed the door of the restaurant. Maybe she should grab something to go. Take home a pile of pasta and garlic bread to eat while she sat on her sofa in pajamas and watched terrible television.

Or she could not risk another trip out into the rain, and based on how the last half hour played out, that seemed like the safer bet.

Mae started the engine and carefully eased out of the lot. The fall of the rain continued, forcing her to keep her wipers on the highest speed to have any sort of visibility as she headed back to Moss Creek. She was about a mile outside town when an odd sound caught her attention.

It was nearly impossible to hear over the noise of the

pouring rain and the high wind that decided to join in halfway home.

The soft thump was steady and seemed to slow as her foot eased off the gas.

No.

There was no way the universe would do this to her. Not tonight.

Not after the day she'd had.

Mae pulled onto the limited shoulder space, squinting through the rain into her side mirror, trying to get a look at the back tire. But between the water running down her window and the clouds making it seem darker than normal, she couldn't get a good look.

So she grabbed her umbrella once again, the drops of water tucked into the folds of the fabric falling all over her dress as she opened the door and stuck it out into the blowing wind. The only way the umbrella was even remotely useful was to hold it at an almost forty-five-degree angle so the wind couldn't blow the rain right against her. Unfortunately that also blocked her ability to see the tire until she was right beside it.

"You've got to be freaking kidding me." It was impossible to control the volume of her voice. Not that it mattered anyway. This was a completely deserted stretch of road. There was no one to hear her yelling like the lunatic this day made her.

No one to watch her kick the damn tire that was the straw that broke the camel's back.

Except the day had one more straw.

A whip of wind caught her umbrella, twisting it to one side so a second gust could hit it full-force, popping it inside out, leaving her standing in the pouring rain, staring at her flat tire.

"Son of a bitch." She swung the ruined umbrella at the ruined tire, smacking it as hard as she could, a line of expletives racing out of her mouth.

Mae was so busy ranting, spitting every questionable word she knew into the ether, that she didn't notice the approaching car until it was nearly on top of her.

Close enough to realize it wasn't a car at all.

It was a truck.

A familiar one.

The driver's door opened the instant the pickup stopped. Mae gripped her umbrella, considering taking it for a second swing, but the set of sneakers that hit the crumbling shoulder dropped her elbows. The headlights dimmed to running lights, forcing her to squint at the change in brightness, trying to confirm her suspicions.

"What in the hell are you doing out here?" The deep voice was exactly what she was hoping not to hear.

Mae blinked a few times, forcing her eyes to adjust. "You freaking blinded me, asshole."

"Get in your damn car." Boone came in close, taking the destroyed umbrella from her hand.

"No." Mae planted her feet, forcing her eyes away from the odd sight in front of her. She'd only ever seen Boone in jeans and boots. Even in high school. That was all he wore. All any of the Pace boys wore.

She shook her head, trying to clear out the distraction of this sportier version of Boone. It didn't matter what he was wearing. He was still Boone.

Still the man who walked out of her life then waited until everything was finally fine to come right back in.

And muck it all up again.

One dark brow lifted. "No?"

She tipped her dripping head in a nod. "You heard me."

Boone's lips eased into the smile that used to make her heart skip a beat. "You're a hard woman to ignore, Mae."

CHAPTER THREE

MAE LOOKED HALF ready to kill him with her bare hands and leave him dead on the side of the road. "Get back in your truck, Boone. I'm fine."

"Didn't say you weren't." Boone opened the driver's door of her SUV and tipped his head toward the interior. "You gonna get in, or you gonna cut off your nose to spite your face?"

Her eyes narrowed at him, long dark lashes sticking together from the rain running down her skin and soaking into the thin fabric of her dress.

He half hoped she decided to be stubborn, just so he could get a better look at the way it clung to her shape.

A shape that wasn't quite how he remembered it.

Mae's chin lifted. "I'm fine. I'm not scared of the rain."

"Doesn't seem like you're scared of much." Boone shook as much water out of the umbrella as possible before working it over and around, popping the supports back into the proper positions before tying it up and dropping it into the floorboard. "Considering you're standing on the side of the road where no one would see you until they were right on top of you."

"You saw me."

She was trying to prove something. And she did.

It just wasn't what she thought it was.

Boone closed the door and stepped closer, taking in the face of a woman where he still expected to see a girl. "I will always see you, Mae."

She stood still as stone, the rain running down her cheeks in streaks of trailing water. "You shouldn't be here."

He wanted to stare at her longer, count all the ways she was different. All the things about her that were new to him.

But she was soaked to the skin, and as much as the long-suffering part of him loved it, the sight of her shivering cut straight to the core of him.

So he passed her, heading for the back end of her SUV. "I was hungry. I went out to grab some food." He opened the hatch. "Didn't know I'd be lucky enough to find you on my way home."

"I don't mean here." Mae pointed to the ground at her feet. "I mean here." She waved her arms around, the pitch of her voice changing. "In Moss Creek."

"Why not?" Boone lifted out the floor panel covering the well holding the spare tire.

"It wasn't good enough for you ten years ago." She swiped at a clump of blonde hair stuck to her cheek. "You don't deserve it now."

"Why do I feel like we're not talking about Moss Creek?" Boone pulled out the spare, dropping it to the ground at his feet before retrieving the bundle of tools and using the wrench to loosen the jack.

"Of course we're talking about Moss Creek." Mae came closer. "We don't have anything else to talk about."

"You sure about that?" Boone rolled the tire toward the side of the SUV. Mae took a step back, getting out of the way.

"I'm positive of that." She stood at his back as he twisted off the lug nuts. "How could we have anything else to talk about? I haven't seen you for ten years."

"You saw me today." He wanted her to remember it like he did. Wanted her to think of every word he said. Every breath he took.

Like he did her.

"At least you showered since then."

Boone chuckled. "I work on a farm, Sweetheart." He pulled the flat tire free, standing up and turning to face her. "I'm not always gonna smell as pretty as whoever you dressed up for tonight."

Mae's eyes widened, making it clear he hit the nail on the head.

She'd been on a date.

One that must not have gone too well considering there wasn't a man following her home.

"Maybe this is how I dress now." She stomped after him as he went to put the flattened tire in the back end of his truck so he could have it repaired. "You don't even know me anymore."

He tossed the tire into the bed. "That's clear as hell, Mae." He turned to face her, immediately stepping close. "But I know you well enough to know you don't dress like this." He let his eyes drift down to where the drenched dress curved tight to the swell of her breasts, daring to linger only a second before dragging them to a more respectable spot.

Mae scoffed. "What about you?" She frowned at him. "What in the hell are you wearing?"

He'd spent almost his whole life living in boots and jeans. First working the ranch with his father and brothers, and then traveling the country as a professional cowboy. It was what people expected of him, and for a long time he was happy to deliver.

Happy to live the life he tried so hard to want.

Her gaze slid down his front. "You don't even look like you."

Boone took in the slope of her nose. The soft sprinkle of freckles across the bridge. "You look just like you."

Mae was different. There was no arguing that point. She'd bloomed from a girl into a full-blown woman. The kind that made a man want to go to his knees and prove his worth. Beg her to be his.

And once upon a time he'd had her. Held her close. Promised her the world.

And then he took it all back. Chose his world over theirs.

Like a fool.

Like a coward.

But she was still every bit as beautiful. Every bit the most desired girl in town.

Woman in town.

He pulled his eyes from her for the second time, forcing himself to do what needed to be done in spite of his complete desire to keep her here as long as possible.

With him.

Boone lined the rim of the spare up and tightened it into place before lowering the jack.

"Why does it look like that?" Mae stood right behind him, arms crossed over her chest.

"Looks like that because you got a flat spare." It was a gift he didn't deserve.

But was sure as hell going to take.

"How can the spare be flat too?" Her words came quick. "It's a spare. That's the whole reason for it."

"Probably just defective." Boone jacked the car back up and pulled the spare off, taking it to the back of his truck and tossing it in to join the other tire.

"So what in the hell am I supposed to do now?" Mae shoved one hand toward the tireless rear end of her SUV. "I can't drive home like that."

No. She definitely could not.

Thank the good Lord.

"Looks like you're going to need a ride."

Her lips pressed tight together. She started shaking her head. "No. No way."

Mae turned and went to her car, flinging open the driver's door.

Boone went to stand beside her, leaning back against the rain-covered side of the SUV. "Whatcha doin'?"

Mae fished her cell out of her purse. "I'm calling an Uber." She swiped one finger across the screen, leaving a streak of water as she went.

"You're going to call someone when there's a perfectly good truck sitting right there?"

Mae's attention snapped to his face. "Nothing about you is perfect or good, Boone."

Ouch.

He shifted, turning to face her. "Let me take you home, Mae. It's late. You're soaked. It's just a ride. That's all."

That wasn't all. Not if there was anything he could do about it.

He'd been home for almost a year.

Twelve months of staring down what he left behind. Twelve months of having to stay away from her, knowing there weren't enough apologies in the world to make up for what he did.

And there still weren't.

Mae glared at her phone a second longer, her expression souring even more with each passing heartbeat.

"How's your service out here?"

She slowly turned to him, teeth clenched tight together. "You know how my service is."

He held one arm toward his truck. "After you."

Mae yanked her purse from the SUV, clutching it to her chest as she stomped past him, not even bothering to keep her words under her breath as she ranted about the rain. Defective tires.

And defective men.

"Not defective, Sweetheart. Everything works just fine." At least it did last time he checked.

Which was longer ago than he'd ever admit to his brothers.

Mae spun to face him, one brow lifted high on her forehead. "Oh, you're defective, Boone." She pointed at his crotch. "But it's not your dick that's the problem." Her finger lifted, stopping right at his chest. "Your issue is in this general area."

She'd stunned him into silence. Not because she called him heartless.

Which she had.

"Did you just say *dick*?"

Mae's full lips pulled into a slow smile that made him both terrified and scarily turned on. "You've been gone a long time, Cowboy. A lot's changed since you left." She pulled open the passenger's door and swung herself up into the seat like it belonged to her.

It should.

Boone raked one hand through his hair, knocking the rain collected there loose.

He tried not to consider the thought of Mae when he first came home, but then during a run-in with Clara's dick of an ex-husband she'd pointed a knife at his chest, and ever since he'd struggled not to think of her.

What it might be like to have her again.

Now he had her.

And didn't have a clue what in the hell to do with her.

The passenger door opened and Mae's head popped out. "Are we going or not?"

Boone fished his keys out of one pocket. "We're goin'. Don't get your panties in a bunch."

"What I do with my panties is none of your business." She dropped back to the seat and slammed the door.

He knew Mae was different. Knew the woman who owned the most successful eatery within twenty miles was not the same girl he left behind.

But this...

This was like a completely new person he was dealing with, and it made it hard to know what to do.

What to say.

How to act.

Boone climbed into the cab of his truck, the scent of his cold dinner lingering in the air.

But even the pasta he'd driven almost thirty minutes to pick up couldn't drown out the sweet hint of flowers and spice coming from the woman beside him.

"Did you at least get something good to eat on your *date*?" The last word came out a little shorter than he meant it to.

Mae didn't turn his way. "I'm fine."

Boone risked a glance her way.

Maybe this Mae wasn't completely different from the one he knew. "Didn't ask if you were fine. I asked if you got to eat."

With Mae it was more about what she didn't say. She was the kind of person you had to read between the lines with.

Before, it was because she held back, not wanting to put anyone out. The Mae he knew was sweet and soft and careful not to step on toes or feelings.

This Mae was not that Mae, in spite of a similar way she had, and it made him wonder why she held back now.

His question was met with silence.

"Take this." Boone passed over the order of lasagna and salad he'd called in.

Mae glared down at the bag. "I don't want your cold dinner."

"Then let me take you to get a hot one."

Mae's head slowly tilted, eyes taking on a look he'd never seen in them before.

She looked angry. Dangerous.

Wild. Like the storm that brought her to him tonight.

"The only place you can take me is home." Her wild grey eyes narrowed. "You've taken me enough places in your life, Boone. I'm not stupid enough to let you take me anywhere else."

Oh, he could take her places. Places he could guarantee she'd never been before.

For twelve months he'd pretended he wouldn't try to get Mae back.

Lied to his brothers.

His mother.

Himself.

Now that lie was staring him in the face. Taunting him.

Testing him.

"Then I'm happy to take you home." He had no plan. No idea how in the hell to come back from where he was.

What he'd done.

All he knew was he had to try.

Because this Mae...

This woman who was a little of what he remembered, but still completely new...

She was all he should have ever wanted. All he should have been man enough to keep.

Mae blinked, straightening in her seat. That's what it was now.

Her seat.

"Good then." She pulled the purse in her lap closer to her chest, holding it tight with both arms.

Boone took his time driving to the diner she lived above. Mae was silent as they turned onto the main road running through the center of town. The Wooden Spoon was in an old three-story building that was one of the original structures in Moss Creek. When he left it was run down and neglected. Now the brick was painted a rich shade of navy. The tall windows of the top two floors were dressed with wood blinds that kept him from ever managing a peek into her world.

The world she built when he took back the one he offered.

Mae didn't wait for him to put the truck in park. She was out the door, slamming it shut behind her and racing to the front door of The Wooden Spoon before he could so much as say goodbye.

It was fitting since he hadn't done it the last time he left her.

This time he stayed, making sure she was inside with the door relocked.

Then he stayed a little longer. Watching as the lights on the second level switched on, their glow illuminating the blinds.

His clothes were wet and sticky. His dinner was cold and coagulated.

It didn't matter.

Boone smiled, shifting the truck into drive as he glanced up in his rearview mirror, tilting it down so he could see the tires in the back.

Mae was going to kill him when she realized what he'd done while she was busy being mad at him for breathing.

She might even hunt him down with that wild look he'd gotten a glimpse of.

His smile widened as he coasted down the street, one hand slung over the wheel as he whistled out a tune.

He was going to figure out how to make everything up to Mae.

Because Mae wasn't the only one who'd changed in the past ten years.

He wasn't the same selfish boy who put himself first.

He was a grown-ass man.

One who was ready to put Mae first.

Every damn day.

CHAPTER FOUR

MAE RACED DOWN the stairs as she heard Camille come in the back door of the diner. "I need you to drive me out to Red Cedar Ranch."

She hit the floor and stopped, feet skidding over the worn wood.

Camille's eyes wouldn't meet hers.

"What the fuck?" Mae took a slow step toward her friend, head tilting as she took in the sight in front of her. "Please tell me that's not what I think it is."

"It's fine." Camille's hand went to the bruised skin of her cheek and temple. "I can take you to the ranch."

"No, no, no, no. That is not fine." Mae closed the gap between them, unable to look away from Camille's face. "Where is the bastard?"

She was going to kill Junior Shepard.

No.

She was going to castrate him. Then kill him.

No.

She was going to use a vegetable peeler on his dick. Then she was going to castrate him. *Then* she would kill him.

"Gone." Camille dug into her purse, pulling out her keys.

"Like, gone *forever*?"

Camille's eyes finally came to hers. "Are you asking if I killed him?"

"No." Mae held her hands up. "Because if you killed him, you should never tell anyone." She widened her eyes, dragging out the next word. "*Anyone*."

"I didn't kill him." Camille walked toward the back door.

"Exactly." Mae hurried to open the door, her eyes lingering on Camille's swollen skin. "He just disappeared."

"No." Camille walked out to the small lot at the back of the building where her car was parked. The same car she'd been driving since high school. "He left when I said I was calling the police."

"You still called them though, right?" For years Mae had seen the signs that Junior might not be as decent of a man as he pretended to be in public.

But never once had Camille whispered a word that he might be hurting her.

"I just wanted him to leave." Camille walked to the driver's side of her car, a slight limp marring her gait.

Mae was definitely going to kill Junior. Murder him in cold blood and feed him to the hogs on Liza's ranch.

Then she would fish through their poop for his teeth and crush them up with a hammer.

Camille started the car, wincing a little as her brows came together. "Where's your car?"

"I got a flat." This morning she'd been pissed as hell when she realized Boone left her high and dry with no way to get her tire fixed. Now Boone was the least of her problems. "What if you come on full-time at the diner?"

"You can't afford to pay me to work full-time, Mae." Camille pulled around the building.

"I can make it work." Whatever it took to give her friend what she needed to leave that scum sucking son of a—

"I'm fine. I'll be fine." Camille's words were calm and even.

And strangely familiar.

Because Mae had said them herself. Many times.

"You and Cal can come stay with me." Mae let out a breath, trying to calm the homicidal rage burning inside her. "I have plenty of room."

"You have an unfinished third floor and a single bedroom." Camille glanced her way. "Cal and I will be fine."

"What if he comes back and tries to hurt you again?" Why was Camille not freaking out over this? Why was she not looking for a deserted plot of land to dig a hole at least six feet deep so the cadaver dogs wouldn't be able to smell Junior's stink?

Mae's belly went cold.

Camille wasn't freaking out because this was old news to her.

The muscles of Mae's throat tightened, making it hard to swallow.

Hard to breathe.

"You can't stay with him, Camille." Desperation lodged in her chest. "He will hurt you again."

Camille stared straight ahead. "I will be fine, Mae. I promise."

"But—"

Camille shook her head. "I don't want to talk about this anymore."

Mae slumped down in her seat.

Maybe she was going about this the wrong way.

Maybe she should kidnap Camille and Cal. Hide them away on her third floor until she could figure out how to make Junior disappear.

By the time they pulled into the drive at Red Cedar Ranch Mae was pretty sure that might be her best bet.

How terrible could the punishment be for kidnapping someone with their best interest in mind?

Maybe not bad.

Definitely worth it.

Mae waited for Camille to shut off the engine. "Aren't you coming in?"

"I have a lot to do at the diner before we open."

She'd secretly hoped Camille would come in and this whole thing would be taken out of her hands.

Because Maryann Pace would be ready to go murdering too if she saw the bruise on Camille's face.

But that would be nothing compared to what would happen if Bill Pace saw.

"I'll be back as soon as I can." Mae grabbed her bag and climbed out. "Thanks for the ride."

Camille gave her a little smile. "Anytime."

Mae swallowed hard as Camille drove away.

Her friend's own issues sort of knocked her anger down a peg. If the worst thing she had to deal with was Boone Pace then she should be grateful.

She turned to face the house where she'd spent more than a little time as a teenager in love. She'd been inside a handful of times since, each one filling her with an odd sense of nostalgia.

And sadness.

Which pissed her off.

Thank God, because right now she needed to be pissed. It was what would carry her through what needed to be done.

Mae marched to the front door. She was just about to knock when it opened and her newest friend smiled out at her.

"Morning." Clara had one of her soon-to-be stepdaughters propped on one hip. "What in the heck are you doing here so early?"

This was not how she'd imagined this trip going. She expected Boone to be here. Planned to yell at him until he returned what was hers.

That meant her answer was horribly lacking. "Boone's got my tires."

Clara's dark brows went up. "Is that some sort of euphemism?"

"No. He's literally got my tires." Mae turned toward the front lot where all the family trucks were lined up.

Boone's wasn't there.

"Boone might still be back at the cabins. You could check there." Clara backed up. "You wanna come in? Breakfast will be up in just a few minutes."

Getting sucked back into the Pace family was not something she wanted to let happen. Mae loved Maryann. Loved Boone's brothers. Loved their dad Bill.

It was one reason Boone leaving the way he did hurt so much. She lost more than just him.

Not that the Paces wouldn't have been happy to keep her on as one of their own.

She was the one who couldn't handle it.

That would involve too much *what might have been* for her to deal with.

"I'm good." Mae backed up. "Thanks, though." She gave Clara a smile. "Are we still on for lunch Thursday?"

"Of course." Clara came to town with the intention of being a nanny for Boone's oldest brother Brody.

Instead Brody convinced her to be his future wife.

Because Brody was a smart man.

And she'd convinced Clara to be her friend.

Because she was a smart woman.

Mae shot her a forced smile. "I'll go find your future brother-in-law then."

Clara grinned back. "Give him hell."

She planned to.

Mae skipped down the steps and went straight for the barn. She walked through the open door and stopped.

She'd been in the house since Boone sent her life on a completely different trajectory than she planned.

But she hadn't been in the barn.

The smell of fresh hay and animal was a shock to her system, taking her back to a time when life seemed so much simpler.

A large head came out of nowhere, bumping into her.

Mae turned, smiling at a pair of big brown eyes lined with long lashes. "Hey." She reached up to rub along the horse's neck. "How are you?"

"Mae?"

She jumped at the deep voice.

Brett poked his head out from the room where they kept the saddles and the rest of the tack. "What in the hell are you doing here?"

She gave the horse a last pat before stepping away. "Where's your asshole brother?"

Brett grinned. "Which one?"

"Don't give me shit. You know which one I'm looking for." In truth Brett was her favorite of Boone's brothers. He was sweet and funny and laid back. "Where's Boone?"

"Boone?"

"Who else would I call an asshole?" At first she'd been heartbroken when Boone told her he was leaving.

When he actually left she was devastated. Broken in a way she didn't expect to recover from.

But she had.

She came back from it better. Stronger. Smarter.

More driven.

Her own person.

It was something she wasn't before.

Not that she was glad he did what he did. He was still an asshole for it. Plain and simple.

"Boone's staying back at the cabins with the hands."

"Why?" The farmhouse was plenty big. More than enough room to house Brody and his twin daughters along with Clara and her son Wyatt while still having room for Boone.

"Ma wouldn't let him stay there when he asked to come back."

Boone *asked* to come back?

"Is he back there now?"

Brett lifted his shoulders. "Prolly."

Well shit. The cabins weren't terribly far, but they also weren't terribly close.

Definitely not walking distance. Especially not when you had a breakfast rush you were hoping to be back in town for.

"You still remember how to ride?" Brett came out of the room with a saddle in his hands.

"I can't ride back there." She hadn't been on a horse in years. Since—

"It's like ridin' a bike." Brett opened the gate on one of the stalls. "I'd take you back there but I gotta get the horses ready for everyone." He led a lean black-and-white-spotted mare from the stall.

"Is that—" Mae's words stopped working as an unexpected amount of emotion clogged her throat.

"No." Brett gave her a soft smile. "Tilly's gone." He and the mare came her way. "This is one of her's though." He stopped in front of her. The mare dropped her head, looking for attention. "This here's Nellie."

Mae lifted a hand, letting it drop back. "She looks just like Tilly."

"Acts just like her too." Brett reached up to pat the horse's rump. "She's easy to ride and sweet as hell."

Mae blinked.

Of all the things to get emotional over, a horse was not anything she would have expected.

She was just tired.

Still mad over Junior and her desire for him to find his way to the bottom of a deep hole.

"Take her out." Brett tightened the saddle, checking to make sure it was secure. "She needs ridden. She's fidgety."

"I shouldn't." Mae stepped back, putting some space between herself and the horse. "I just want my tires."

"Go get 'em then." Brett walked Nellie down the center of the barn and out the door into the yard, leaving Mae standing alone.

All she wanted was her tires.

The tires Boone stole from her.

Brett stuck his head back through the door. "You comin'? She's gettin' impatient."

Hell.

Mae stomped her way to the door. She wasn't the kind of woman who stood by and let life happen.

Not anymore.

She grabbed it by the balls and made it what she wanted.

She decided how it would go.

And right now that meant getting her damn tires back so she had a vehicle to move a body.

Just in case the situation presented itself.

Mae tightened the cross-body strap on her purse as she walked, huffing out a breath as excitement tried to wiggle its way into her belly.

There was nothing to be excited about. This was just to get what belonged to her so she could go on with her life.

The life she created. Grew.

Owned.

Brett stood back as she grabbed the saddle and went up and over, settling into place. She tipped her head his way. "If you see your brother before I do, tell him I'm coming for him."

Brett grinned. "Happy to pass the message along."

She nudged Nellie with her heels and the horse

immediately started moving in an easy gait. Mae turned to where Brett stood.

He pointed toward the east, where the sun was just peeking over the horizon. "Head that way. She'll get ya where you're wanting to go."

This morning's trip to Red Cedar Ranch wasn't really about wanting. It was about doing what had to be done.

And what had to be done was putting Boone Pace in his place.

Last night he definitely had ideas, and she was here to quash them.

Murder them the way she wanted to murder Junior Shepard.

Mae reached out to stroke along the horse's neck, trying to calm the upset turning her stomach.

Nellie's gait was even and smooth, making the ride an easy one. As easy as it could be considering she was about to face down the man who nearly broke her.

Split her into pieces that never went back together the same way, leaving her different than the person she used to be.

Maybe better.

Not that she'd ever tell him that.

Nellie eased in the direction of the row of small buildings set next to another barn. A handful of men were moving around the area, pulling out horses and drinking coffee. She'd only been past the cabins a few times in the four years she was with Boone. Mae's eyes drifted to one side, lingering in the direction of a part of the property she was more familiar with.

Was it still the way she remembered it?

Probably not. Nothing ever was.

Nellie picked up the pace on her own, moving faster as they got closer to the cabins. Mae lifted her butt, working to move with the mare to avoid a bruised ass. She urged the horse a little more.

Might as well enjoy something about this day.

The moving air caught her hair and made her eyes water in the most wonderful way, easing away the sickness still pulling at her belly from the sight of Camille's bruised face.

She could be upset about it again later.

But right now she needed this moment.

This freedom.

It was short lived.

Nellie slowed suddenly as a familiar truck came into view, heading down the gravel drive leading from the main house to the cabins.

Mae pulled Nellie to a stop, staring across the field as Boone parked his truck and climbed out looking much more like himself than he had last night. He stood tall and broad, one hand moving to tip back the brim of his hat.

The sound of a whistle carried through the morning air.

Nellie immediately started moving, picking up speed even as Mae tried to stop her.

The mare ignored every attempt she made.

"Come on, Nellie Girl." Boone's deep voice made the extent of the Pace brothers' dedication to each other clear.

And Brett used to be her freaking favorite.

Nellie went straight to Boone, pushing her face into his outstretched hand the minute they got close.

He grinned up at Mae. "Mornin'."

"You have my tires."

"You have my horse." Boone turned his attention to the mare in question. "Did you take good care of her, girl?" He passed a treat to Nellie even though her care would qualify as biased at best.

Boone's eyes lifted her way. "You comin' down?"

"I haven't decided yet."

His brows lifted. "You stay up there and someone'll put you to work."

"I'd rather work up here then be down there with you."

Boone grinned, not looking even a little deterred by the jab. "I'm sure come lunchtime there'll be a whole herd of hands that'll appreciate your sacrifice."

Damn.

She promised Camille she would hurry back.

"Ugh." Mae swung off Nellie, not even bothering to look as she kicked her leg up, over and down.

Maybe she looked a little.

Boone caught her ankle before her foot could come close to clipping him. The sudden stop threw her off balance and sent the rest of her dropping down the side of the horse.

Right into Boone's waiting arms.

CHAPTER FIVE

HE'D BEEN UP all night planning out how he was going to handle this morning.

Mae falling right into his arms was never even on his radar.

But here he was, holding her for the first time in a decade.

Unfortunately he was the only one who was happy about it.

"You did that on purpose." Mae wiggled free, flailing her arms around as she fought for balance on the uneven ground. She stomped a few feet away, spinning in place, the wildness back in her eyes as she looked him up and down. "You and freaking Brett."

"Not sure how Brett fits into this." His youngest brother was more than ready to take on the responsibility of a wife and kids, but he knew Mae was strictly off the table.

Mae pointed one finger straight at Nellie. "He's the one who put me on your damn horse."

"He knew you loved her momma. Probably figured you'd like gettin' to know her too."

"Well I wouldn't." Mae wiped one hand across her forehead and straightened her spine. "I just want my damn tires back." Her expression softened. "I need to get to work."

"Then let's go." Boone turned, clicking his tongue as he walked toward the barn where Nellie normally stayed. The horse immediately started following him, ready to go back to her usual space after a night of being in the family barn so he would have one less thing to mess with this morning.

Her stall was clean and ready and he made quick work of putting her up. Once everything was in place he went outside, half-expecting Mae to be gone.

The sight of her standing next to his truck, arms crossed, deep frown turning down the sides of her mouth, did something to him he wasn't ready to think on too much. "Let's go get you put back together."

"I'm not broken, asshole." Mae yanked open the passenger's door, swinging up and into the cab like she'd done it a hundred times.

She had.

It used to feel like a lifetime ago. Now it felt like a different life all together.

One that he remembered well.

And she wanted to forget.

Boone settled into his seat, forcing his eyes ahead instead of letting them go to Mae. She'd probably gouge them out at this point.

"I'm sorry."

"You should be. I had to make Camille drive me out here

this morning. Screwed her day all up." The line of Mae's mouth was tight as she glared out the windshield.

"How's Camille doing?" Camille was the youngest of the Smith girls and the only one married. She'd made the mistake of hooking up with Junior Shepard in high school and ended up pregnant. Rumor had it Junior did it on purpose, trying to trap the girl who was head and shoulders above anything he should ever have been able to land. But Camille was young and didn't have a clue how shitty Junior could be.

Boone worried for years she'd find out.

Mae's whole body went tight. "She's fine."

This time Boone let himself study her, but it wasn't for her own benefit. "If Junior's acting up I'm happy to put him in his place."

Mae turned toward the window, hiding her face from him.

But she didn't hide her next words. "His place is a hole in the woods."

Boone took a deep breath, taking the time to choose his words carefully. Unfortunately it was easier said than done, so he settled on the only one he could manage. "Yup."

Mae's head snapped his way. "What's that mean?"

"Means he's always been a son of a bitch." Junior was in Brody's class in school and the rumors around him didn't stop at his successful attempt to knock up Camille.

"How do you know that?" Mae and Camille were the same age. Young enough to have missed out on Junior's previous bad behavior.

"Brody's been itching for a reason to kick Junior's ass

since one of his old girlfriends came to school with a black eye junior year."

Mae's lips flattened to a thin line. "Brody can't go around kicking people's asses. He's a father."

Boone rolled his shoulders, trying to ease the tension collected there. "Not sure that would stop him under the right circumstances."

"What would the right circumstances be?" Mae's purse settled a little lower as she softened the double-arm hug she had on it.

"I'd say there's more than a few." Boone turned to face her. "The main one being if he found out Junior hurt Camille."

"Oh."

"It's probably worth noting that things would be different if Junior hurt Cal."

"Different how?" Mae's tone only carried curiosity and it settled him a little.

Boone faced the road for a second before once again finding her eyes, holding them with his. "Then Junior would be begging to be put in that hole you mentioned."

Mae's gaze held his. "You'd have to find him before I did."

He never expected the hypothetical murder of a man to be what they bonded over first, but he'd take it. "I'd let you help."

One of Mae's brows lifted. "What makes you think I wouldn't be the one letting you help?"

Boone smiled in spite of the darkness of the conversation. "I'm always at your service, Mae."

"Hmph." She turned away, clearly less impressed by his offer than he'd hoped.

But he wasn't ready to give it up just yet. "That's why I took your tires."

She tipped her face his way, offering him a side look. "You took my tires because you want to service me?"

He blinked.

Did she mean that the way it came out?

There wasn't a hint of blush on her cheeks. Not an inkling of shyness in her eyes.

"I will take every opportunity to service you, Sweetheart." The sight of Mae's SUV on the side of the road in front of them threatened to cut the conversation short, severing the first real connection he'd managed to have with her since coming home.

Mae huffed out a sigh, pursing her lips to one side and wrinkling her nose. "I don't think I'm so interested in your services. They were pretty amateurish last time I checked out what you offered." She opened her door and jumped out, leaving him sitting in the truck.

Mouth hanging open.

Amateurish?

He was fucking nineteen the last time she experienced his services for Christ's sake. What did she want from him?

Mae was at the back of his truck dropping the tailgate by the time he caught up with her. "At least I knew where the clit was."

Part of him was hoping to shock her the way she'd shocked him. Back in the day Mae was a little bashful when it came to discussing...

Services.

"You want a fucking award for understanding female anatomy?" She grabbed the tire, fighting it toward her.

"Congratulations. You know the absolute basics of how to get a woman off."

Basics?

"I'm not a damn nineteen-year-old kid anymore."

She lifted her brows, pausing in her struggle with the tire. "Well you still act like one."

The tire dropped free and she rolled it to where her SUV was still jacked up and ready.

"I do not."

She snorted as she crouched down and grabbed the tire.

"Give me that." Boone moved in at her side, gripping the repaired tire and lifting it into place. "Stubborn woman."

"Being self-sufficient makes me stubborn?" Mae shoved at him with her shoulder as she tried to push him out of the way. "I can put my own tire on."

"I'm sure you can, but you shouldn't when I can do it for you." He pressed back, being careful not to knock her over.

"Cause why? Now you want to take care of me again?"

The hurt edging her words cut into his hide, slicing with a precision nothing else could.

Boone dropped his head and stared at the ground.

When he came home it was clear the best he could hope for was to find a way to coexist with Mae in Moss Creek. He knew Mae was single, his mother made sure to torture him with the fact every chance she got, but thinking there was a snowball's chance she could ever forgive him was a fool's dream.

And somehow in the past twelve months he'd become a fool.

"I shouldn't have left you."

Mae was silent for a minute. Finally she shrugged one shoulder. "It doesn't matter now, does it?"

"It does matter." It always mattered. Even when he didn't know it did.

"You had shit you wanted to do." Mae stood up, moving away. "It's fine. I get it."

She didn't get it. Not even a little bit.

Hell, it took him years to get it.

And even longer to admit it.

Boone pulled the lug nuts out of his pocket and threaded them into place as Mae paced along the other side of the SUV. Her phone rang and she answered it, giving short, single-word answers as her pacing sped up.

"Yup."

"Almost."

"No." The *no* carried a level of disdain that hinted at the question preceding it.

Boone tightened the last nut into place and lowered the SUV to the ground.

Mae turned as the vehicle settled to the ground. "I'll be there in ten minutes." She tucked the phone into her purse as she came his way. "What do I owe you for the tire?"

"Nothing."

Her nostrils flared. "I don't need your charity, Boone."

"Then make me lunch tomorrow." He backed toward his truck, hoping she wouldn't notice he hadn't replaced her spare. "I'll come pick it up and we can call it even."

She crossed her arms. "You're awfully trusting to eat food I make for you."

He grinned. "What can I say? I'm a trusting guy."

Mae was many things. Angry. Proud. Stubborn.

She was also honest and hard-working and she would never do something that would make her business look bad.

Like using it to poison her scumbag of an ex-boyfriend.

Even if he deserved it.

Boone climbed into his truck and waited, making sure Mae made it onto the road before pulling out behind her and following her into town.

Her eyes came his way in the rearview more than a few times and each one bolstered the idiot inside him.

The one who believed he might have a chance with Mae and was ballsy enough to keep trying in the face of overwhelming evidence to the contrary.

She turned into the lot at The Wooden Spoon, her SUV slipping out of sight as she left him to continue on his own.

Fitting.

By the time he got back to the ranch everyone was out for the morning, working at their designated posts. He'd skipped breakfast in his haste to get Mae's tire into town so his friend could plug it and replace her faulty spare. Now his stomach was as growly and pissy as he was feeling.

Boone peeked his head into the back door of the house, listening for any sign his mother might be nearby.

She'd been spending most of her time out at The Inn, preparing for their grand opening, which took a little of the heat off him. Freed up his movements around the house.

Made it easier to raid the fridge without having to face the third degree.

Boone had a hunk of turkey shoved in his mouth and an apple in his hand when his scavenging was interrupted.

"There's some pie in there that's real good."

He leaned around the door to peek at Wyatt. "That's 'cause your Mimi makes the best pies."

Wyatt shook his head. "Nu-uh. Mae does."

Well hell. There was no fucking escaping her around here.

Boone grabbed the pie plate from the fridge and bumped the door closed. "Which one's your favorite?"

"Cherry." Wyatt didn't even have to think on it.

Boone grabbed a couple plates and went to the table. "She put the crumbles on the top or more crust?"

Wyatt shrugged. "Depends on the day."

"Which one's better?" Boone scooped out some of his mother's apple pie onto a plate and pushed it toward Wyatt.

Wyatt did have to think about it this time. His brow furrowed as he forked off a chunk of the chilled dessert. "I think I like the crust one best." His lips curved into a sheepish smile. "Mae puts extra whipped cream on it too."

"That sounds like her." Boone shoved in a big bite of the pie that now seemed lackluster in comparison to what he might have if he could figure out how to get back into Mae's good graces. "She's a pretty good cook then?"

Wyatt's big brown eyes moved around the quiet kitchen. He leaned closer, his voice low. "She's even better than Mimi."

"Good." Boone polished off his pie and went to work on the apple. "What's on your schedule for the day, Little Man?"

"Dunno." Wyatt shrugged. "My mom's up putting the girls to sleep so I'm just trying to be quiet."

Boone leaned back in his chair, watching as his nephew plowed through his serving of pie. "You wanna go out for a ride with me? I've got something I need to check on."

Wyatt smiled wide. "Sure." He shoved in his last bite of pie as he jumped up from the table, racing to the sink with his plate.

"I got that." Boone took his own plate to the sink, starting the water as he tipped his head toward the hall leading to the front of the house. "Go make sure it's okay with your momma."

Wyatt nodded and took off on quiet, but hurried, steps.

Boone washed their dishes and put away the rest of the evidence of their mid-morning snack. By the time he was done Wyatt was back, hat and boots in place, ready for their ride.

"I think you were meant to be a cowboy, Little Man." Boone tipped the brim of Wyatt's hat. "Ready?"

They spent the next few minutes saddling up Wyatt's horse, Abigail. Once Wyatt was situated, Boone went in search of a horse for himself. The family barn was mostly empty, with the exception of Penny, a mare who just weaned her foal. He stopped just outside her stall. "You feel like gettin' out, girl?"

Boone got Penny saddled up and smiled as the horse got more restless with each passing minute.

"Is she okay?" Wyatt watched from his spot atop Abigail, eyes squinted with concern.

"She's ready to get going." Boone mounted up, settling into the borrowed saddle. "She's tired of being a stay-at-home mom and is ready to get out and have some fun."

Boone set a decent pace he knew would make Penny happy but that Wyatt could comfortably handle. The little boy was getting better and more confident with each passing day and the last thing he wanted was for a mishap to set him back.

They rode for nearly a half hour before Wyatt turned to look his way. "Where we goin'?"

Boone pointed to a grove of trees that just came into sight. "Over there."

As the trees got closer his concern deepened. In the center of the cluster of firs and honeysuckle stood a huge oak tree.

One he'd been trying to save since coming home.

Wyatt stared at the same spot. "That's a big tree."

"It is." It was the biggest tree on their property as far as he knew.

"What's wrong with its leaves?"

"It's got a fungal infection." Boone led Penny into the grove, easily navigating through the familiar space.

"That's sad."

Boone turned to Wyatt. "It is sad." He reached out to pat the little boy on the back. "I've been trying to save it, but it just keeps getting sicker." Boone dropped to the ground and walked to where the leaves of the oak were scattered around the place he thought of more than any other. He reached down to pick one up as he stared toward the upper branches of the tree.

"Is it gonna die?" Wyatt stood beside him, looking up at the same spot.

Boone reached out to rest one hand against the trunk of the tree. "I hope not."

CHAPTER SIX

"HELLO GIRLS."

Mae dropped her head down to peek out the service window toward the dining room. Maryann Pace's smiling face beamed back at her. She offered back as much of a smile as she could manage. "Hey, Maryann. How are you?"

"I'd be better if I could find someone to run the damn Inn." Maryann's eyes drifted, peeking into the kitchen through the narrow window.

"You wanna come back here?" The offer was out before Mae could stop it.

"I'd love to." Maryann was gone from the window and appearing through the door almost instantly. She tucked to one side as one of the waitresses came past with two baskets of bread. She glanced to where Camille was at the prep table, working her way through some of what they needed ready for tomorrow. Her eyes stayed on Camille as she walked toward Mae. "You don't have anyone on staff you'd be willing to part with, do you?"

Mae looked to where Camille was working. "To be the general manager of The Inn?"

Maryann nodded. "It would be full-time." Her eyes came to Mae and stayed. "With benefits."

Full-time.

And benefits.

Why had this not occurred to her earlier?

Boone. Because Boone. He was frying her brain.

"Camille." Mae blurted out her friend's name and had zero regrets about doing it. "I'd hire her full-time if I could, but I don't have an opening right now."

She technically didn't have the part-time opening she'd given her.

Maryann leaned closer. "Do you think Camille would be interested?"

Definitely. "Possibly." Mae glanced to her friend. "You'd have to ask her."

Maryann's lips curved into a soft smile. "Maybe you girls can come out to the ranch after you close up tonight. I'm sure she'd be more comfortable coming if you were there too." Maryann backed away. She paused, lifting a finger. "And she should bring Calvin. I'm sure Wyatt would love to have someone his own age to play with."

Mae shoved on a smile.

No good deed.

"Great."

Maryann smiled wide. "Excellent."

Mae watched as the matriarch of the Pace family went out to join her husband and granddaughters at their usual table.

"What was that about?"

Mae jerked at the closeness of Camille's voice, turning to where her friend stood looking out at the Pace family. "Maryann wants us to come over tonight with Calvin so he can play with Wyatt."

Camille's brows came together. "How did you get lumped into that?"

"Maryann thought you might be more comfortable with me there." Mae passed over a prepped plate of the day's special as one of the waitresses came to retrieve it. "She wants to talk to you about running The Inn."

"What?" Camille's skin paled. "I don't know how to run a place like that."

"Liar. You've been working here with me almost a year. You've seen how to manage a staff." Mae grabbed a plated club sandwich and fries, checking it over and sprinkling a finish of minced parsley over the top before passing it through the window. "And what you don't know I can teach you."

"I've worked here six months, not a year. That's nowhere near enough time to know how to do everything—"

"You don't need to know how to do everything." Mae snagged the next lunch that came her way. This one was the soup of the day in one of the freshly-baked bread bowls The Wooden Spoon was known for. The center of the steaming serving of beef with barley got a dusting of chives and sent to its waiting table. "I will help you." Mae took advantage of the temporary lull in plates to turn to Camille. "You need this. You need to have options."

Camille held her gaze. "Junior doesn't want me working anywhere full-time."

Maybe Junior wasn't as stupid as she thought. "Cause he

knows you'll leave his ass." Mae kept her voice low. Word in Moss Creek could travel fast and she didn't want anyone alerting Junior to the possibility that the woman he swindled into marrying him might have one foot out the door. "I'm even willing to risk having to look at Boone for this."

Camille sighed as she turned to stare out at the dining room. Her lips slid into a sly smile. "Seems like you won't have as long to wait on that as you were thinking."

"Wha—" Mae followed Camille's line of sight.

She shouldn't have said his name out loud. He was probably like freaking Rumplestiltskin.

An angry little goblin who showed up where he wasn't wanted to ruin women's lives.

"He never comes here." Camille turned to eye Mae. "You think he's here with Maryann and Bill?"

"No." She'd hoped he wouldn't hold her to this. Prayed Boone knew what was good for him and would stay away.

He stopped right in front of the window, not even looking Mae's way. "Hey, Camille."

Camille smiled wider than a good friend would. "Hey there, Boone. What brings you here?"

Boone seemed relaxed, but his eyes were focused as they rested on Camille's face, skimming over the heavily made up spot where a purple bruise hid. "Came for the lunch Mae promised me."

Camille's mouth gaped a little before lifting back into a smile. "That was awful nice of her."

Boone's blue gaze shifted to Mae. "Wasn't it?" He braced one arm against the top of the opening between them, leaning in a little more. "I'm ready to finally try some of the best food within fifty miles."

Mae crossed her arms. "Only fifty miles?"

He grinned at her. "As the crow flies, of course."

"Of course." Camille started to back away. "I should probably get back to work."

Mae turned to her supposed friend, twisting far enough Boone wouldn't see the widening of her eyes.

Camille didn't slow her retreat down even a little.

"So what do I get to pick from?"

Mae huffed out as she turned back to Boone. "No one said you got to pick anything." She tipped her head toward the line. "Someone pack Mr. Pace a lunch special up to go."

"So I get a *special* lunch then."

She rolled her eyes at him. "Ha-ha."

"You don't have double-crust cherry pie today, do you?" Boone glanced to the spot where his mother and father sat with Brody's twin daughters. "It's Wyatt's favorite and I thought—"

"You thought maybe I'd throw a piece of pie in for you too?"

Boone's gaze snapped her way. "I thought maybe you would send a piece for him to eat after school." Boone's face came closer, lining up with hers from the other side of the opening in the wall between them. "I don't intend to take anything you won't willingly give me, Mae."

The thought of giving anything else to Boone Pace should make her sick.

Make her mad at the very least.

Except neither of those were the reaction she had to his words.

"Here you go." One of the line cooks landed a bag on the counter beside her and rushed away.

Mae pushed the package of food through the window. "I'll make sure Wyatt gets some pie."

She needed him to leave and she needed him to do it now. Mae dropped her eyes to the plates lining up in front of her, focusing hard on adding the finishing touches as she prayed Boone hadn't seen the thoughts that just ran through her traitorous bitch of a mind.

"Mae?"

Don't look up.

Don't look up.

Her eyes lifted, meeting the blue gaze she used to get lost in. "What."

Boone was silent for a minute. Long enough to make her horrible heart skip a beat in anticipation of what he might say next.

"Thank you."

"Yup." She dropped her eyes again, ready to focus on anything besides Boone and the awful, terrible reaction she just tried to have to him.

Mae checked and topped the plates waiting to go to the dining room, passing them over without looking up, unwilling to risk another look at him.

Once the counter was clear she dared a peek.

Boone was gone and the tiniest ache tried to twinge in her chest because of it.

But he wasn't the only Pace she had to worry about.

Maryann caught her eye from across the room, a look that could best be described as cautious irritation settled across her striking features.

Mae shoved on a smile as fast as she could.

Boone hadn't technically done anything wrong.

This time.

Maryann's head tipped in what almost looked like a nod as her eyes slowly moved to the man at her side, leaving Mae to go back to what she was supposed to be doing.

Living her life.

One that didn't involve the Pace family. Not anymore.

———

"CAN I RIDE a horse?"

"Not today." Camille turned to look at Calvin where he sat in the back seat of Mae's SUV. "We can't stay too long."

Cal's face fell. "Okay."

Mae pulled her eyes from where she was watching him in the rear view mirror. "I bet you can come here again sometime, though."

"We'll see." Camille turned to face forward, her posture tense as she stared out at the land around them. "I'm not sure this is a good idea."

"You have to do something." Mae turned onto the long gravel drive that led back to the main house. She snuck another peek at Cal. He was still paying just as much attention to them as he had the whole drive. "There has to be some sort of alteration made."

"What are you altering?" Cal's little boy voice was soft and careful.

"A pair of pants that she should have thrown away a long time ago." Mae tried to keep away the sour expression any mention of Junior put on her face.

"Is Mrs. Pace gonna help you with the pants?" Cal was

usually a quiet kid, but he'd been abnormally chatty on the drive out to Red Cedar Ranch.

"I'm not sure, honey." Camille twisted the strap of her purse. "Probably not."

"I really think you should let her help you with the pants." Mae lifted her brows and shot Camille a look. "Or I could help you with the pants." She pulled into the only remaining spot left in front of the house. Cal immediately piled out, stopping to stare at the house in front of him.

"I can't do this." Camille shook her head. "I can't." She blinked a few times as she sucked in a shaking breath.

Guilt tugged at Mae's belly. She'd pushed her friend too hard. Been so excited for something that was probably terrifying for Camille.

Change was hard whether it was good or not.

"I know this isn't how you saw things going." Mae smiled a little as a happy black dog bounced his way toward a laughing Calvin. "It sucks when your life doesn't end up the way you thought it would, but you have to suck it up and make it what you deserve for it to be."

Camille sniffed a little. She nodded.

"You wanna go inside and just hear what she has to say?"

Camille was quiet for a minute, her hazel eyes moving along with her son as he ran around the grass, the big dog hot on his heels. "Okay."

"Okay." Mae waited for Camille to open her door before following suit. Just as she stepped out onto the gravel a sharp whistle and yell cut through the air. Calvin immediately stood stock straight, his eyes wide and filled with something that made Mae's insides turn to ice.

Fear.

Mae looked Camille's way but Camille was focused only on her son.

On his reaction.

"*Duke.*" Brett Pace stepped out of the barn, cowboy hat tipped back as his clear blue eyes searched the yard. It took them all of two seconds to find Camille, then two more to find Calvin. His face split into the easy grin that normally occupied it. "Hey there, partner." He tipped his head to the black dog circling Calvin's feet. "I think my dog likes you."

"This is your dog?" Calvin cautiously reached down to pat Duke's head, his eyes never leaving Brett.

"Sure is." Boone's youngest brother slowly ambled Calvin's way. "His name's Duke."

"That's a good name." Calvin eyed Brett as he came closer.

Once Brett was at his side he immediately crouched down, scratching Duke behind one ear. "I'm Brett."

"I'm Calvin." One finger shot out Camille's way. "That's my mom. She's coming to see if Mrs. Pace can help her fix some bad pants."

"Bad pants, huh?" Brett's eyes moved Camille's way. "I bet there's lots of people round here happy to help her fix those pants."

Camille's eyes went wide, but Brett's attention was already back on Calvin.

"You want to come help me feed the horses while your mom decides what she's going to do with the pants?"

Calvin looked to Camille. "Can I?"

Camille rocked on her feet a little. "If Mr. Pace is sure you won't be in his way."

"He will never be in the way around here." Brett stood,

pointing to the open barn door as he smiled at Cal. "Go on in there and get acquainted." Calvin made a beeline, but Brett took the long way to the barn, coming past where they stood on the driveway, his eyes holding Camille's. "And I think I'd prefer for him to call me Brett if that's okay with you."

Camille's hands twisted at the strap of her purse again. "Whatever you're more comfortable with."

"I want you to be comfortable with it too. He's your son." Brett's voice was softer than normal, his drawl a little slower.

Camille's gaze was wary as it moved over Brett. "It's okay with me if it's okay with you."

The smile he gave Camille was softer than the wide grin he'd offered her son. "It's more than okay with me." Brett tipped his head toward Mae. "I believe my momma's inside waiting to feed you girls some dinner."

Camille's eyes followed Brett as he went to the barn. "You think he'll be okay?"

"He'll be better than okay." Mae knew exactly what it was like to walk into the world of Red Cedar Ranch. She'd come from a happy home and it was still like stepping into a magical world.

She could only imagine what it was like for Cal. "He's never going to want to leave."

Wyatt came running out of the barn, Calvin hot on his heels as they raced toward the large fenced-in run connected to the hen house that supplied the eggs Maryann fed to the hands every morning.

"I'm not sure that's any better of an option." Camille's cheeks puffed as she blew out a long breath. "Let's get this over with."

Her steps only hesitated a little when Maryann came out

on the porch wearing a warm smile she directed straight at Mae and Camille.

Mae fell back a little as they climbed the steps to the porch. Maryann immediately wrapped one arm around Camille's shoulders, leading her straight into the front door, sealing Camille's fate whether she knew it or not.

Camille walked right into the Pace family orbit. Once you were there, the gravitational pull was inescapable.

Unless of course it was one of them who spit you out.

CHAPTER SEVEN

"DID SHE TAKE the job?" Boone sat at the small round table in Brooks and Brett's cabin.

Brooks lifted his shoulders as he tipped back a bottle of beer, taking a swig before answering. "Not sure."

"She should." Brett frowned across the table as he organized the cards in his hand. "She needs to be able to get the fuck away from Junior."

"Maybe she doesn't want away from Junior." Brody tossed out a card.

"Why wouldn't she want away from Junior?" Brooks glanced up at Brody, eyeing his euchre partner a little too long.

"No cheating." Boone tossed out his own addition to the round.

"That boy of hers is too jumpy." Brett's frown turned to a scowl as he continued moving the cards pinched in his fingers. "Looked like he almost shit himself when I hollered for Duke."

"Probably 'cause Junior's just as likely to be screaming at

someone as he is to be drunk." Brooks dropped a card to the pile at the center of the table. "And he's always fucking drunk."

Boone tapped one foot against the floor, working out the anger making him want to open his mouth.

But telling his brothers about the bruise he saw, peeking out from under the layer of makeup Camille slathered on in an attempt to hide it, wouldn't do anyone any good.

They'd all end up in jail.

Brett was already three beers in. More than enough to forget what happened when they showed up at a house uninvited to teach someone a lesson.

After the fun part.

"You gotta let her do what she needs to do." Boone swallowed down some of his own beer, hoping it would temper his desire to rid Camille of her problematic husband. "She needs to decide what she wants. All we can do is help make sure she has plenty of options."

"That what you're doing with Mae?" Brooks glanced his way. "Making sure she knows she has plenty of options?"

Boone kept his eyes on the cards. "Mae has any option she wants and she knows it."

Mae didn't strike him as the kind of woman who accepted things the way they were. She was the kind of woman who made shit happen.

Like resurrecting a building that should have been demolished and turning it into the best restaurant Moss Creek had ever seen.

"Heard you got lunch at The Wooden Spoon today." Brook's lips teased a smile. "Kinda surprised to see you here tonight. Figured you might have ended up with food poisoning."

Brett's brows lifted. "You ate at The Wooden Spoon?"

Boone knew the second he saw his mother and father sitting in the diner that he was made. "I helped Mae with a car problem. She offered to pay me and I took payment in pot roast."

"Hell." Brody swiped his hand across the cards, collecting the round and stacking it beside him. "Now you're really gonna be stuck on her."

Boone held out his hands. "Are you eighty years old? No one says *stuck on her*."

"Fine." Brody leaned in, eyes right on Boone. "Now you're really gonna want to see just how different Mae is than you remember."

"That what you're tryin' to do?" Brooks looked from Boone's cards to his face. "Get back with Mae?"

"I was drivin' home and she was stuck on the side of the road. What did you want me to do? Leave her there?"

"I mean," Brett finished off his beer and tossed it to the can in the corner, "you did steal her tires."

His brother's eyes all came his way.

"She watched me put them in the back of my truck." It was technically true. It was also technically true that Mae wasn't paying a lick of attention to anything that night outside of making sure he knew how much she despised him. "And I gave them back."

He gave one back. The other one he was planning to use as an excuse to see her again.

Because Brody wasn't wrong.

He was stuck. Had been for years.

And it had nothing to do with pot roast.

"Mom'll kill you if she thinks you're trying to get with Mae again." Brody's brows were up as he took the next round.

"I'm almost thirty fucking years old. I'm not living my life based on what my mother thinks I should and shouldn't do." Boone shoved up, going to the fridge for another beer.

"I'm not saying you shouldn't do it." Brody held his hand out, indicating he wanted another beer. "I'm just making sure you know what'll be coming for you."

He knew. Their mother hadn't hidden her displeasure with him.

Boone popped the caps off the beers, passing one off as he sat down. "Not so sure it matters anyway."

His chances of winning Mae over were slim to none. He shouldn't even be entertaining the idea.

But he couldn't seem to help himself.

Maybe it was self-inflicted punishment. Torturing himself for what he did to her.

"I mean," Brooks gave his head a little shake, "she's still single after all this time so that's something."

"And it's not because she doesn't have options." Brett tossed out a trump card and collected the round. "Every man in town has tried to get her at one point or another, and she's never taken a single one up."

"She was out on a date the other night." Boone offered it up as evidence that Mae wasn't as lonely as his brothers wanted him to believe.

As he wanted to believe.

"Maybe she's just not into cowboys then." Brody grinned. "Maybe she's had her fill."

"Or maybe she's tired of everyone in town trying to hump her leg." Boone slapped his next card down as he mentally ran through the names of the men who most likely tried to snag Mae. "She's fuckin' busy."

"She'll be busier if Camille takes that job." Brooks added one more round to his and Brody's collection, effectively taking the majority they needed to win the game. "Which she hopefully will."

Brody leaned back as he downed the last of his beer, standing to toss the empty bottle in the recycling can. "I gotta go. I told Clara I wouldn't be too late."

"At least one of us is going home to a warm bed." Brooks collected the cards and stacked them together.

"There'll probably be kids in it by the time I get there." Brody pulled off his hat, raking one hand through his smashed hair before setting it back in place. "The girls are even worse about sleeping in my bed now than they were."

"Not sure I can blame them on that one." Brett managed to dodge the throw pillow Brody snagged off the couch and launched his way. "I mean because Clara's a good mom. Shit. Calm the fuck down."

"I'll kick your ass, Brett." Brody was already half out the door.

As the door closed behind him Brooks turned Brett's way. "He's never gonna get over you trying to call dibs on her."

"You'd of done it too if you saw her first." Brett leaned back in his seat, kicking his boots up onto the seat of Brody's vacated chair.

Brooks leaned back, attention going to Boone. "What are you going to do about Mae?"

"Why do I have to do anything about Mae?" He wasn't so

interested in disclosing his intentions with Mae. Even to his brothers.

Brooks snorted. "Come on. We'd have to be blind not to see that you're kicking the hell out of yourself for walking away from her."

"You should." Brett pointed Boone's way. "She was a hell of a girl when you were with her and she's only gotten better since you've been gone."

That was what bothered him the most. The one thing that made him think he should leave well-enough alone.

He'd learned the hard way that his life was better with Mae in it.

But maybe Mae was better off without him in hers.

"She's accomplished a lot in ten years." More than she would have with him in the picture.

"She owns that building, know that?" Brooks sounded proud as he laid out how Mae secured a loan on the building and built The Wooden Spoon from the ground up, introducing Moss Creek to a different kind of eating experience. "Until she opened shop everyone around here thought the best way to eat bologna was on Wonder bread."

He'd heard about Mae's leveled-up diner fare, but so far he hadn't been lucky enough to try anything but the best pot roast he'd ever had.

"Maybe you should give her another flat so you can try some more of her cookin'." Brett grinned.

Boone stood. "Not sure it's a good idea for me to try to get anything else from Mae."

"Right." Brooks didn't sound convinced. "You'll leave Mae alone when pigs fly."

"I'm goin' to bed." Boone opened the door and left.

Talking about Mae and how well she did without him soured his mood.

Not that it was great to start with.

Knowing she was at the ranch with Camille and that he had to stay away from her had him antsy and irritated. He'd been hoping a card game and beers with his brothers would help, but all it did was make things worse.

Add on that he was headed to a cold, lonely single bed and he was about as pissy as possible.

By the time Boone laid his head on the pillow, there was no more denying any of his intentions where Mae was concerned.

And they were adding up.

Because winning Mae over was the least of his problems.

Mae wasn't the same girl he once had.

So he had to prove he wasn't the same anymore either.

————

"WHAT ARE YOU doing here?" Mae didn't glance up as she rushed to get through the line of plates on the counter in front of her.

"Came to give you the replacement spare." Boone peered into the kitchen through the narrow window. He'd come at an off hour thinking maybe Mae would be less busy. "I can come back another time."

"Just leave it in the lot beside my car." Mae shoved two plates onto the stainless-steel shelf between them as a waitress bumped into him.

The waitress gave him a sheepish smile. "Scuse me."

"Sure thing." Boone moved down, giving the waitress room to collect her plates.

It took longer than he was expecting.

Mae's eyes went to the young woman as she continued to work Boone's way and he continued to back up. Her brows snapped up. "Food's getting cold, Cecily."

Cecily grabbed the plates, her smile still mostly on Boone. "Sorry." She sauntered away, peeking back his way over one shoulder as she headed to a table where an older couple sat holding hands.

"She's single." Mae passed another plate through the window.

Was that a hint of jealousy in her voice?

Boone turned to study what he could see of Mae through the opening. "Good for her."

"You should ask her out." Another plate came through the window, this one carrying a little more force behind it.

"Not interested in asking her out." Boone came here thinking this would go the same way it always did. Mae would make it clear she hated him and he would try to make her change her mind.

This was an unexpected surprise.

"Why not? She's clearly interested in you." The next plate nearly slid over the edge, forcing Boone to stop it with his hand to avoid losing it to the floor.

"I got my reasons." He carefully lined the plates in a neat row for the waitress coming his way. He scanned the packed dining room. "Busy day."

The waitress coming to retrieve her plates was the mother of one of his high school friends. She lined the dishes down one arm. "And we're short-staffed." The second the last meal was in place she was gone again, hustling to a table crowded with hands from Cross Creek.

Another happy surprise.

He turned to Mae who was head down again, trying her best to keep up with the food flying from the kitchen. "Anything I can do to help?"

She snorted. "Sure. You wanna come wash dishes?"

He didn't give her the chance to take the offer back, immediately going to the swinging door and bumping his way into the kitchen.

Mae's thunderstorm eyes were wide on him. "What? No. You can't—"

"You just said I could." He pointed to the line of steel sinks across the back wall. "I'll be back there if you need me."

That was the key. Finding some way to prove he had worth to a woman who'd gone out of her way to prove that he was worthless.

That she could provide for herself. That she could be more without him.

She'd succeeded and it made a guilty part of him proud.

He deserved no amount of pride for what Mae'd done. None of it belonged to him.

But he was still so damn proud of her.

The sinks were stacked with bussed plates. Bowls hinting at the soup that once filled them.

And flatware. Hundreds of pieces of flatware.

Boone went to work sorting and stacking, coming up with a plan to attack the mess Mae would have been left with. He filled one deep sink with hot soapy water and the next with hot clear water and started scrubbing. By the time the kitchen behind him started to quiet down he was almost halfway through the mess, cleaning, rinsing and racking up one plate after another.

"If you weren't a cowboy you'd be one heck of a dishwasher." Cecily came to lean against the line of sinks.

"Seems like." Boone turned to glance Mae's way, catching her chilly gaze where it rested on Cecily. A second later it flicked to him before immediately snapping away.

"I'm Cecily." The waitress scooted closer.

Boone sent the bowl in his hands through the rinse water before propping it into the rack.

"You're Boone Pace, right?"

"Yup." He scrubbed at a particularly stubborn bit of cheese.

"I've always wanted to ride a horse." She smiled. "I bet it's real fun."

"You should find my brother Brett then. He's always looking for a riding partner." Boone tipped his head Cecily's way. "If you'll excuse me." He left her standing there and headed straight for Mae, moving close enough to her that it would be clear to anyone looking where his interest was. "You got time to get that tire now?"

"You in a hurry to get on with your plans for the day?" She peeked Cecily's way under her lashes.

"I'm in a hurry to get your tire taken care of so I can come back and finish your dishes." He eased a little closer. "Then maybe I'll mop your floors."

Mae's eyes lifted to his, narrowing. "I don't need your help, Boone. I'm just fine on my own."

"Didn't say you weren't." Boone reached out to snag a bit of something green caught in a wisp of blonde hair falling from the thick braid laced down the back of Mae's head. He gently pulled it free, turning it her way. "Parsley?"

Mae looked at it then at Boone.

She reached up and pulled the leaf from his finger, her skin brushing his for the first time in a decade. She rubbed the bit of bright green between her fingers then sniffed it.

"Cilantro."

"That the stuff that tastes like that dishwater I been working in?"

"Cilantro is amazing." Mae dusted the herb free of her fingers.

"I'm going to have to disagree on that."

"You've just never had it in the right thing,"

Yet another gift from what was turning out to be a fine day. "Probably not since I'm not welcome in the best place to eat in town."

"I thought it was the best place in fifty miles." Mae's lips teased him with a hint of a smile. "As the crow flies."

CHAPTER EIGHT

SHE SHOULD NOT be flirting with Boone Pace.

Hell, she shouldn't be talking to him at all.

"Guess I don't really have enough to compare for me to lay my reputation on that claim." His smile was slow and easy. Different from what she remembered.

"Why do I feel like you're trying to get lunch out of me again?"

"I like to think I've earned it." He tipped his head to the sinks at the back of the kitchen. "That's a lot of dishes I'm doing."

Mae sighed, her head falling back. "Fine."

"Do I get to pick what I eat this time?"

"You're pushing your luck." She untied the apron covering her front. "Come on." Mae went to the back door where her car was parked in the small lot reserved for her and her employees. Boone glanced up the stairs leading to her apartment but didn't say a word as they passed.

She stopped and stared at the giant red truck parked

across the back of her SUV. She turned to Boone and lifted a brow.

He ambled past her. "How was I supposed to know I'd end up on KP duty?" He reached into the bed and pulled out the spare.

"This is a private lot." Mae clicked the button to unlock the doors of her car. "You could get towed."

"By who?" Boone opened the back hatch and lifted the cover on the well where the tire went.

"Not everyone is as forgiving about your abandonment of Moss Creek as I am."

Boone turned to look her way over one shoulder. "This is you when you're forgiving?"

"I haven't pulled that door down on your head, have I?"

Boone's face split into a wide grin. "I guess I should say thank you then." He straightened, pulling down the door and closing it into place. His blue eyes went to the back of the building before scanning the lot. "Where's Camille?"

Mae pressed her lips together, working them across each other. "She texted me this morning to let me know she couldn't make it in today."

Boone leaned against the tailgate of his truck. "She okay?"

"Probably."

Boone studied her a minute, making her work to stand still.

If Boone knew—

"I saw that bruise on her face, Mae. You're the only reason I haven't gone over to teach Junior what happens when you put your hands on a woman." The tone of his voice sent a shiver down her spine.

A shiver that landed right in her belly and stuck there, warming a little more with each passing second. "I'm not sure what I have to do with that."

Boone came her way, boots eating up the blacktop between them. "Cause I promised when I went after him I'd let you help." He didn't stop until he was close enough she could almost feel the heat from his body.

Close enough she should step back.

Close enough to ease the tightness that started squeezing her chest when Camille texted her this morning. "I can't make her leave him and it sucks." Mae swallowed at the lump in her throat. "He's such a piece of shit."

"It will happen, Mae. I promise." Boone was suddenly even closer, the scent of clean man and leather soothing her more than it should. "She's just got to know she can do it. That she's strong enough."

"She is strong enough." It almost came out as a yell. The frustration. The helplessness all built together and made her feel a desperation no amount of deep breathing could calm.

Boone's hands came to rest on her shoulders, warm and solid and strong. He leaned down, holding her eyes with his. "She will figure it out, and when she does we will be there to make it happen."

His eyes were so blue. Bluer than she remembered. A little darker.

More serious.

Maybe it was because of the conversation.

Or maybe that was who he was now.

As much as she'd tried to keep thinking of him as the boy who left her behind, taking all the promises he'd made with him, right now there was no denying that Boone Pace changed.

Grew into a man. One she was struggling to hate in spite of herself.

"Okay." Mae sniffed in a deep breath. "But I get to throw the first shovel of dirt on him."

"You can throw the second shovel too." Boone's hands slowly came off her shoulders, their weight and heat a loss she felt immediately.

"Thanks." Mae reached up to tuck some stray hairs behind one ear. "Um. Do you know what you want to eat?"

"I can think on it while I finish those dishes." He opened the back door, holding it for her. "Or you can surprise me."

"Okay." She was out of sorts. Discombobulated.

It was just because of the day. Camille wasn't the only one who didn't make it in today, and the entire morning and afternoon had been hectic and stressful.

She was just tired. That was all.

Mae went inside, watching from the corner of her eye as Boone walked straight to the sinks and started scrubbing like it was his job.

"You want me to finish the prep for tomorrow?" Rayne, one of her best line cooks, tilted her head. "You okay?"

"I'm fine." Mae waved the question off. "I think we're okay. You can go ahead and go." Rayne worked her tail off today trying to make up for the lack of hands in the kitchen and there was no way Mae would force more work on her. "Thank you for your help today."

"Sure thing, boss lady." Rayne gave her a fast smile. "See you bright and shiny."

Mae turned, heading to check on the status of the dining

room. They were set to close up in an hour. The last food left the kitchen at 2:00. She'd learned early on there was no way to juggle breakfast, lunch, and dinner without making herself absolutely crazy.

And breakfast and lunch had all her favorite foods. For the people who loved dinner food, she did one special a day that fit that bill. Today was chicken à la King. Tomorrow was beef stroganoff.

Which meant she had to prep all the beef and mushrooms tonight, along with the rest of everything else that had to be done.

"How are we on bread?" Mae went to Carmen's station.

"We are good." Carmen gave her head a shake as she cut a pile of risen dough into bread-bowl-sized portions. "I'm on the last of it."

"If they eat any more than they already are we won't be able to keep up." At this point it took all the capacity they had to bake the bread and pies to be used the next day. There simply wasn't the room or time to make any more.

"Then they'll have to deal with it." Carmen shrugged. "They want bread, they'll get here early."

"Do I just put a sign on the door?" Mae rested one hand on her head. "*Sorry. No more bread.*"

"I can have Jim make you a sign." Carmen's husband was a hell of a handy guy. He'd made the sign for the diner along with a number of the tables and chairs inside.

"Tell him I'll send him a pie." It was the only part of the cooking she still handled all by herself. Everything else had been delegated.

But the pies were the one thing she couldn't manage to let go.

Speaking of.

Mae went to her own little spot of the kitchen, pulling the stacks of chilled dough from the fridge and lining them along the counter before going to work. Tomorrow's pie was an unfortunate choice all things considered. She dug out the peaches she'd sliced and brown sugared earlier, draining all the accumulated juice into a measuring cup before adding in spices, bits of candied ginger, oat powder, and minced pecans. She mixed a few spoonfuls of cornstarch into the collected juice before pouring it back over the peach mixture. By the time Carmen was done with the ovens Mae's pies were lined up and ready to go in.

She normally went through fifteen pies a day.

On peach pie day she went through twenty.

Mae waved at Carmen as the older woman left for the day, giving her a little smile as she turned toward the hot ovens, a pie balanced on each upturned palm.

"This place cleared out fast." Boone stood at the rack of dishes, wiping the last plate dry with a dish towel.

"It was a crazy day. They're probably all ready to get the hell out." Mae went straight to the ovens and started sliding pies inside. "I would have thought you'd be right there with them."

"Is that what you would have thought?" Boone set the final plate on the stack he'd spent the afternoon scrubbing down. "Cause I made it pretty clear I intended to stay until the work was done."

"The work's done." Mae closed the door on the last of the pies. She'd spent a small fortune on the kitchen at The Wooden Spoon, betting on herself and her ability to make this place the success she knew it could be.

And she'd been right.

After five years of busting her ass and pinching pennies, the loan her parents put their house on the line for was all but paid off.

Her kitchen ran like a well-oiled machine.

Usually.

The tables were always full and they always sold out of bread and pie and whatever the day's special was.

She had everything she promised herself she would.

It was supposed to feel good.

She was supposed to be happy.

Fulfilled.

Up until a year ago she thought she was.

"Doesn't seem like the work's done." Boone tipped his head to the ovens. "Seems like you've still got work to do."

"Those are for tomorrow." Mae scanned down the line of dishes Boone washed, dried, and stacked. "And you've done more than enough."

"Not sure I'd call a few dishes more than enough." Boone's nose twitched as he leaned toward the line of ovens. "What kind of pies are those?"

"Did you decide what you wanted for lunch?" She turned from the smell of baking peaches.

Why did she even make peach pie? She shouldn't have ever baked one again, let alone dedicated a whole day to it.

And unfortunately it didn't end there.

She'd spent hours perfecting it. Proving she made the best peach pie in existence.

Partly out of spite.

The rest of the reason was something she never let herself admit.

"I heard through the grapevine you make a good bologna sandwich."

"You want me to make you a bologna sandwich?"

Boone leaned against the counter. "I will be happy with anything you're willing to give me, Mae."

The odd feeling of offness came back full-force. She'd been able to ignore it while she worked, but without pies to distract her, there was no avoiding it. "Okay." She turned to the line, looking down the cleaned counters as her brain struggled to decide where to begin.

Was there a place to begin?

"I can help." Boone reached to the stack of pans stashed away, pulling one free. "This the right size?"

"It's a little big."

He turned the handle in his palm, sending the large pan spinning. "Not for two." Boone set the pan on the cooktop. "Pretty sure I'm not the only one who skipped lunch."

"I usually don't eat until everything's finished." Mae went to one of the freshly-baked loaves of bread and set it on the slicer, closing the plastic door and pressing the button, sending the blades through the crust of the multigrain loaf.

"Not even breakfast?" Boone's eyes were on her as she lined four slices down the counter before tucking the remainder into a clear plastic sleeve.

"Depends on the day." Mae went to the cooler and pulled out the stick of bologna. She grabbed a knife on her way back.

"Hmph." Boone crossed his arms.

"Hmph?" She sliced off two thick pieces of the bologna and laid them in the pan before switching on the flame under them. "Not all of us have a full breakfast waiting on us every morning."

"You *own* a place that makes breakfast every morning." Boone came to stand right beside her. "How hard would it be to find a piece of toast and a fried egg?"

"I'm busy."

"You still have to take care of yourself."

Mae slammed the knife down on the counter as she turned to face him. "Don't talk to me about taking care of myself, Boone. I've had a lot of other shit to take care of."

"Because I left."

"No." She huffed out a breath. "Yes." A year ago everything was simple.

She hated Boone. He'd left her.

She'd picked a new life. One that she was in charge of.

Then he freaking came back, which was bad enough.

But now he kept showing up, mixing the life she had with the memories of the one he promised her.

And it was fucking up her mind.

Mae turned to face him. "I expected my life to be one way and then suddenly it wasn't. I had to decide what that meant for me, so I did. My parents put everything on the line to help me. If I didn't succeed they would lose their house. There are people who need the money I pay them. If I don't show up every day then their families suffer." She shook her head. "I can't just run off and do what I want."

"Like I did." There was an oddness to the tone of his voice. The set of his jaw.

"Yeah." The air left her chest and for the first time in ten years she didn't feel angry at Boone. "Like you did."

"I was selfish."

"You were."

"I was a coward."

"That too."

"I was a fool."

"I'm not going to disagree with you."

Suddenly Boone was very, very close. Closer than he'd been. "I walked away from the only thing that would ever matter to me."

Her throat swallowed all on its own. "What?" The single word whispered out.

"I wanted to come home so many times, Mae." He eased in a little more. "But I knew you hated the hell out of me." His front almost touched hers. "And I knew that if I was in Moss Creek I'd come for you again. I knew I would chase you until the day I died." His eyes were dark as they moved over her face. "Even though it's clear as hell you're better off without me."

"But you did come home."

His lips softened into a hint of a smile. "Maybe I'm still selfish."

Her heart raced as his body pressed into hers, the long line of his tall frame warm and solid. "What are you doing?"

"Risking my life." His head tipped, the brim of his hat shadowing his eyes.

"I wasn't really going to stab you."

"Liar." The tips of his fingers skimmed up the sides of her arms with a touch so gentle she could barely feel it. "You were absolutely going to stab me."

"Not today I wasn't."

The smile that teased her earlier peeked out. "Maybe tomorrow then."

"Probably tomorrow."

"It's a date." His touch traced up the sides of her neck, sending goosebumps racing over her skin.

She couldn't look away from his eyes. They were dark and focused and...

Dangerous.

All of this was.

Mae forced her gaze from his, turning away from Boone and the touch she didn't want to enjoy.

"What's wrong, Mae?" There wasn't a trace of upset in his tone.

Just concern.

And that might be the most dangerous part of it all.

She barely peeked his way over one shoulder, not trusting herself to fully look at him again, as she snatched a spatula from the rack. "The bologna was burning."

CHAPTER NINE

MAE HADN'T STABBED him, so that was good.

And she hadn't knocked him on his ass for touching her.

Also good.

He should be celebrating small victories, but right now all he could think about was the kiss he'd been so close to.

"Could you watch this while I get the rest of what we need?"

We.

A single word that soothed the lingering disappointment he didn't deserve to have.

"I will do whatever you need me to." Boone slipped the spatula from her hand, letting his fingers drag across hers, stealing another touch of her skin.

"I'll remind you that you said that." Mae opened the cooler and pulled out a container of creamy spread and a box of lettuce leaves. She came back to his side and started assembling the sandwiches, spreading some of the brown-tinted mayonnaise across each slice of bread before stacking a lettuce leaf and a slice from a tomato she'd snagged from a crate on two of the bread pieces.

Mae pointed to the opposite slices. "Put the bologna on those." She went back to the cooler and traded the lettuce and spread for another container.

Boone checked the underside of the bologna slices, making sure they were done before sliding them onto the empty bread.

"Be careful." Mae peeked at him under her lashes. "I might start making you cook your own lunches when you show up."

"I'll remind you that you said that." He gave her a smile.

"Using my words against me?" Mae flipped the tomato and lettuce tops onto the bologna bottoms before slicing them in half and adding each completed sandwich to a plate. "You want potato salad?" She flipped off the lid of the new container and scooped out a serving of the side dish as she eyed him.

"Of course."

Mae lifted her brows. "Interesting."

"Is it?" Boone took the plate as she held it out his way.

Mae shrugged. "You didn't used to like potato salad."

It was the perfect lead into the thing he had to prove to her. "Things change."

"Some things change." Mae's lips flattened into a thin line. "Some don't."

His heart sank.

Mae grabbed her own plate and headed toward the empty dining room. "I think I'm going to go check on Camille tonight."

The sink of his heart turned to dread as it fell to his gut. "I think you need to be careful."

Mae turned, finally looking him in the eye again. "I think Junior Shepard needs to be careful."

"I don't disagree." Boone slid into the booth Mae stopped at, waiting for her to ease into the seat across from him. "But Junior doesn't like when people get in his business." Boone waited for Mae to look at him again. "And I don't think I need to tell you what will happen if Junior lays a hand on you."

"He put his hands on Camille."

"And he will get what he's earned from that." Boone leaned in. "But if Camille isn't going to leave him then me going out there and kicking his ass will only make her life worse."

"I don't want to kick his ass." Mae picked up half her sandwich and took a big bite. "I want to kill him." She chewed her bite, brows up, not an inkling that any part of her was kidding in the expression on her face.

"I feel like if I tell you killing Junior's off the table you'll take my lunch away."

"You might end up getting stabbed after all." She jabbed her fork into the potato salad on her plate. "Why won't she just leave him?"

"It's not always that easy, Mae. Not everyone is like you."

Her eyes lifted to his. "How am I?"

"Independent." He bit off some sandwich. "Strong. Confident you can do anything you have to do."

Mae's chewing slowed. She swallowed, her eyes hanging on his. "I wanted to prove I was fine."

"You don't have anything to prove to anyone, Mae."

"I wanted to prove it to *you*." She said the words slow. "I wanted you to see that I was fine without you."

"I might argue you're better without me." Her accomplishments were easy to see. They sat right on Main Street for all of Moss Creek to look at.

And none of it would have happened if he hadn't left. Hadn't forced her to choose another plan for her life.

"But you're still here." One side of her mouth lifted. "Trying to win me back."

Her bluntness took him by surprise. He hadn't been real secretive about what he was doing, but he'd expected her to ignore it at least a little longer.

Shows what he knew.

"I'd be a fool not to."

"Maybe you're a fool for trying." Mae polished off the last of her sandwich, dusting her hands together over the empty plate in front of her.

"I'm a fool for a lot of things, Sweetheart. Tryin' to win you back will never be one of them." Boone snagged her plate and stacked it on his, ready to change the subject before she told him to stop chasing her. "You got a good reason you can think up to go out to Camille's house?"

Mae's brows came together. "I was just planning to go over there."

Boone stood, taking their dishes with him. "That's not gonna end well for anyone." He went to the sink and twisted on the hot tap.

Mae followed him in, her soft presence noticeable the second it came into the kitchen. "I could say she forgot something here and I was bringing it to her."

"Like?" He scrubbed their dishes clean while Mae stood at his side, arms crossed, brows pulled together.

"Ugh." Mae's head fell back. "Why can't we just go there to visit?"

"*We* can't go there at all." As potentially bad as Mae showing up unannounced was, Mae showing up with him at her side was about a thousand times worse.

If Junior didn't know they were onto him already, he would then.

"*You* are going to go to Camille's house." He rinsed the dishes off. "*I* am going to park my ass in the back of your SUV just in case Junior decides to show his ass."

"And if he does?"

"Then you might get to see him end up in a hole after all." Boone racked the last of their utensils and turned to Mae, edging in close. "Because I will skin and gut any man who even thinks about touching you."

"Your sweet talking could use some work."

"Don't try to lie to me, Mae Wells. I may not know you like I used to, but I still know you well enough to recognize that threatening to murder Junior Shepard makes you happier than anything I've ever said to you."

"Most of what you said to me turned out to be a lie." Her words carried none of the vitriol he was used to.

"I'm not so sure it was a lie, Mae." He eased closer. Now that he'd had his hands on her it was hard as hell not to want to do it again. "I think maybe my timeline was just wrong."

"Maybe you had your chance."

"If that was true you wouldn't have almost let me kiss you earlier." If she could be straight with it then so could he.

No more pretending. No more trying to edge his way in by flying under the radar.

"I didn't though."

"And you regret it." Boone crept in a little more, expecting Mae to ease away, put more space between them.

And he'd give it to her.

He'd give her anything she needed. Whatever it took to make this what he'd spent more nights than he could count wishing for.

But Mae's feet didn't move.

The only thing about her that budged was the tip of her chin as she faced him down. "You really think trying to kiss me twice in one day is a good idea, Cowboy?"

"I've never been one to live my life based on good ideas." He rested one hand on each side of where she leaned against the counter. "If I was, then you'd be chasing my babies right now instead of standing in this kitchen."

Her soft inhale was Mae's only reaction to a fantasy he'd played over in his mind countless times.

The life he should have chosen.

Mae at his side. Their babies growing like weeds as they ran around the ranch with Leah and Michaela and now Wyatt.

"I should have picked you, Mae. And once it was done I thought there was no going back. So I didn't come back." She deserved the truth. Even if she didn't believe it.

And that's what he expected. For Mae not to believe him.

"You should have picked me."

Her agreement set him back a step mentally. Kept him from following her words up.

Not that he could have, because Mae kept going.

"All I wanted was to be a good wife to you. A good mom." She huffed out a little laugh like she couldn't believe what she once was. "And I wonder if I would have been happy just being those two things."

"You would never have been just those two things, Mae." It was something that was becoming more clear to him with every second they spent together.

Mae could never have been just anything.

She was always going to be more.

And he wanted her to be his more.

Mae's eyes moved over his face. "I don't know what to think of you, Boone Pace."

"I'm just happy if you think of me."

"Hmph." Mae chewed her lower lip like she was pondering something. "Are you really going to go with me to check on Camille?"

"You're sure as hell not going there alone."

More lip chewing.

Mae took a deep breath. "Let's go then."

"You decide what she forgot?"

Mae reached for a large knife.

Boone snagged it, pulling it out of her reach. "Yeah. Gonna have to say that's a hard no on that one."

"Whatever." Mae looked around the space, lips pushed into a pout that made it even more difficult not to keep trying to kiss her. "I'll go grab a shirt or something."

Boone leaned against the counter as Mae hurried to the back stairs, disappearing up the well to her private living quarters. Hopefully someday soon he could go with her.

See the rest of the life she built all on her own.

Her steps were heavy as she came down the stairs. Mae

held up a shirt, smiling. "I have our new work shirts. She didn't take hers with her yet."

"Perfect." Boone waited as she fished out her keys.

"Don't they need you at the ranch?"

"We just mucked out all the stalls, so right now I'm not in high demand."

Mae's nose wrinkled. "Why are you the one mucking the stalls?"

"You're not the only one upset with me for leaving, Sweetheart." He pushed open the back door, holding it wide so Mae could go out into the back lot where his truck was still parked across the backside of her SUV.

Mae looked at his truck and then at him. "You're lucky you worked here today."

"I'll keep that in mind." He fished out his keys, unlocking the cab before jumping in and quickly moving the truck to the spot just beside where Mae was parked. She was already inside with the engine running. He climbed into the passenger's side, working to get his legs into the small bit of leg room.

Mae watched him, a smile playing at her lips. "I guess you can scoot the seat back."

He tipped his head at her. "Thank you."

Mae turned her attention to the lot as she pulled out. "I forgot how much space you take up."

Boone stretched his legs out as he pressed the button on the side of the seat. "There's plenty of room for me. Just got to do a little reorganizing."

"I thought you were hiding." Mae turned out of the back lot and onto Main Street, turning toward Camille and Junior's house.

"You didn't want to chauffeur me around, did you?" Boone tipped his head toward the back seat. "I'll get in the back once we get closer."

"That should be interesting to watch." Mae shot him a glance, her eyes moving down his body. "You're probably going to get stuck."

"I've crawled into a backseat once or twice in my life."

The flush of her cheeks made it clear Mae remembered exactly when he'd done it.

"Is that really what you want fresh in my mind right now?" Her gaze came back his way. "The things we did in the backseat of my car?"

"I've gotten better at it."

"My standards have gone up." She smirked. "A lot." Mae made the turn onto the unlined road leading to the rundown house Junior's parents bought him when he managed to get Camille to marry him.

"Glad to hear that." Boone shifted in the seat, snapping his buckle loose before reaching between the seats and hefting himself through. "I'd hate to think a teenage boy was the best you'd ever had."

He didn't actually want to think about any of it, but it occurred to him that the more experience Mae had, the more she'd be able to see what he saw.

That they wouldn't ever have what they did before.

But they could have something even better.

The row of seats went all the way across, leaving him to tumble over them to get to the back area where he could hunker down.

Gravel smacked up against the undercarriage as Mae

turned into the drive at Junior's place. "Junior's car's here." Mae sounded a little apprehensive for the first time.

"You got nothin' to worry about, Mae. Just go in. Give Camille her shirt. Make sure she and Cal are okay, and then get your ass back in the car. It's just a quick stop."

"I know." She snapped it out. "I just didn't come prepared to have to dig a hole, that's all." Mae parked the SUV and shut it off. "Want me to crack a window for you?"

"I want you to check on your friend and hustle your ass back out here." Boone slid down. "And you should probably stop talking."

"Ugh." Mae's door opened then closed. Her steps ground into the rocks and got fainter and fainter.

Boone sat perfectly still, straining to hear anything.

It was silent.

He fought the urge to lean up to peek out the window. If Junior saw him out here there'd be all sorts of problems to deal with.

And he had other things he wanted to spend his time doing. Mostly figuring out how to get Mae to let him show her all he'd learned over the past ten years.

Just as his mind started to wander, things went from quiet to chaos.

Screaming. Yelling. Cussing. Banging.

All of it at once.

He immediately went for the back hatch, fumbling around for the handle to open the damn thing.

There was nothing there.

Boone spun to the front, stalling out at what he saw through the windshield.

Mae faced Junior down on the unrailed front porch while Camille and Cal hunkered together at her back.

The wildness he'd once craved was there in her eyes.

But this time it sent a chill down his spine.

Because wild wasn't what was in Junior's glassy gaze.

It was crazy.

Boone gripped the back seats, propelling himself forward just as Junior's hands reached for Mae, grabbing her arms with a white-knuckled grip.

He fought the back door as Junior's fingers dug into Mae's skin as he lifted her up.

And threw her over the edge of the porch.

CHAPTER TEN

THE SON OF a bitch shoved her off the porch.

Mae flailed around in the bushes, trying to get some traction so she could climb back up there and kill Junior like she should have done to start with.

An odd thumping barely registered as she fought her way free of the evergreens, keeping one eye on Junior as he advanced on Camille and Calvin. "Don't you freaking dare." Mae managed to get some momentum going, using it to roll to one side.

Unfortunately it landed her face down in the dirt.

Before she could get her hands under her the thumping from before changed, turning lighter.

It almost sounded like footsteps.

She lifted her head just as Boone launched over her, his long body flying straight at Junior's pudgy one. The impact took both men to the porch floor. Mae jumped up, spinning to grab Camille and Calvin. "Get him in the car." She shoved her friend and her little boy toward the steps, using her body to block Calvin's line of sight so he wouldn't see what was unfolding on the porch.

Cause Junior Shepard was about to get what he had coming to him.

Part of it.

"Was that Boone?" Camille turned as they ran, trying to get a look at the man pummeling her future ex-husband into dust.

The urge to turn was strong. Make sure Boone was as okay as she knew he would be.

But getting Camille and Calvin someplace safe was the most important thing.

Sirens wailed in the distance.

Mae's head snapped Camille's way. "Did you call the cops?"

Camille's eyes were wide. Her head shook.

"I did."

Camille's gaze dipped to the little boy between them.

Calvin's chin quivered the smallest bit. "I didn't want him to hurt you again." His face crumpled a little more. "I'm sorry."

Camille pulled her son close, holding him tight as a line of tears edged her eyes.

Mae turned to the house, dropping her purse and the shirt still clutched in her hand to the dirt at her feet. She marched her way back toward the porch where Boone and Junior were still wrestling across the scuffed floorboards. She stomped up the steps, picked up the closest thing she could find and pulled it back, waiting for a clear shot at Junior's skull.

Cause one way or another he was going to get what he had coming to him. All of it now.

Boone's blue eyes caught hers and a split second later he was free of Junior and coming her way. He snatched the metal table from her, yanking it free just as Junior got on his feet.

And landed a right hook.

Boone swung the table, hitting junior right in the ribs with enough force to break at least a couple.

A second later there were cops everywhere. Enough to make it clear they sent everyone Moss Creek employed.

Two grabbed Junior and two grabbed Boone.

"No." Mae lunged for him. "He didn't do anything wrong."

"I can't breathe." Junior was wheezing, making a show of it that could earn him an Emmy.

"That's 'cause you're a fat, lazy wife beater." Mae looked for something else to swing at him since one of the cops had her last weapon.

"Mae." Boone's voice was sharp enough to steal her attention his way. The spot where Junior managed a cheap shot was starting to swell, squinting up one of his eyes. "Get Camille and Calvin someplace safe."

"But you didn't do anything wrong." Mae stepped toward him again.

"I'll be just fine, Sweetheart." He tipped his head toward Camille. "Go."

She turned to where her friend stood, holding her son tight, watching as they cuffed the man who didn't deserve either of them.

Mae narrowed her eyes at the cop holding Boone. "You

better treat him right, Grady or I'll never let you in The Wooden Spoon again."

Officer Evans huffed out a breath. "You can't blackmail the police, Mae."

"Withholding a freaking bologna sandwich is considered blackmail?"

He gave her a little grin. "It is if it's your bologna sandwich."

Boone eyed Grady with his good eye before turning it to Mae, the brow over it lifting.

"That bitch came here starting shit." Junior was sputtering as he screamed in the face of the officer trying to cuff him.

Mae turned his way. "You're projecting pretty well for someone who can't breathe, asshole."

Junior smirked at her, the blood from his busted lip tinting his teeth as it widened on Boone. "Can't believe you're fuckin' her again, what with it not being good enough to stick around for the first time."

Boone lunged, dragging Grady along with him as he went for Junior again, both hands cuffed behind his back. Grady managed to rein him in before he got close enough to do damage.

And Boone would have done damage, there wasn't a doubt in her mind on that.

"Calm your tits, Pace." Grady fought to keep his feet planted as he struggled to get Boone in check. He leaned in close to Boone's ear. "Right now this is just procedure, Don't make me have to make it more than that."

Boone's jaw set. His face snapped Mae's way. "Go."

She'd never seen Boone mad. Not as a kid and certainly not as a man.

It scared her. Not because she was afraid of him.

She was afraid for him.

"Okay." The less Boone had to be upset about the better, and Junior already knew exactly which buttons to press.

Mae held his gaze a second longer before turning and hurrying to her car. Camille and Calvin were in the backseat, huddled together. She glanced up at her friend in the rearview mirror. "Do you need to get anything else?"

Camille had a bag packed when Mae got there. She'd walked right in on Camille leaving Junior. It already wasn't going well and was only downhill after that.

"I just want to go." Camille's tone was flat. Emotionless.

Mae gave her a little nod. She was at a loss for words.

What do you say in a situation like this?

"Do you want to stay with me?" Mae turned out of the driveway, taking one last look behind them. Boone stood tall, watching her go.

"I have a place to live lined up." Camille smoothed across Calvin's dark blond hair.

"Just tell me where to go."

Camille was silent for a minute. Finally her eyes found Mae's in the mirror. "Maryann's."

———

"I WANT TO talk to him now." Mae glared across the counter at Grady. "I don't care who's talking to him."

"He's gotta give a statement, Mae. That's how this works." Grady rubbed his eyes. "We can't mess this up."

Mae eyed the man she'd known since they were kids. "What's that mean?"

"Means this is a situation that didn't surprise anyone, and we want to be sure there's no wiggle room." His brows lifted. "Make sense?"

One of the other officers came out of a room. He glanced Mae's way. "Glad you're here. Saved me a trip." He came to the counter, pulling out a lined sheet of paper with places to fill in the date and room for a signature at the bottom. "We need a statement from you too."

"Where's Boone?" He'd probably saved her ass today and she owed it to him to save his back.

"For the love of God just let her see him." Grady fell back against his chair. "She's not going to quit asking until we do."

Mae crossed her arms, cocking a brow at the officer she didn't know as well as Grady. "He's right."

"Fine." The officer handed her the paper and a pen as they walked toward the back of the station, past a line of smallish rooms. "Fill this out. Anything that might be relevant." He stopped at the last door on the right, holding one arm out. "There you go."

Boone sat on a small sofa in what appeared to be a break room. He held an ice pack to the eye Junior managed to injure.

Because of her.

He stood. "Mae."

The officer he'd been talking to stood. "I need to go check on a few things." He ducked past where Mae stood in the doorway. She glanced back toward the other officer, but he was nowhere to be seen either.

"What are you doing here?" Boone's voice dragged her attention back his way.

She thought she knew why she was here.

It was supposed to be because he looked out for her and she was trying to do the same.

Out of obligation.

But being here didn't feel like an obligation.

Being here didn't feel like it was for Boone's benefit at all.

"Are you okay?" A hint of a bruise peeked out around the ice pack. Mae stepped into the room, trying to get a better look at the damage Junior inflicted while Boone was preventing her from being the one in handcuffs.

His mouth lifted a little on one side. "You worried about me, Mae?"

"No." She pulled the strap of her purse a little tighter to her body as she looked around the room. "Where's Junior?"

"He's at county." Boone's good eye studied her. "They're going to need to talk to Camille."

Mae lifted the paper in her hand. "I figured." She set the paper down on the circular table wedged between a fridge and vending machine. "At least they didn't make her do it right then."

"They know where to find her."

"Are they going to need to talk to Calvin too?" The thought of Camille's little boy having to recount what happened today broke her heart all over again.

"He'll be okay."

She sniffed at the running of her nose. "I hope so."

"What about you?"

Mae adjusted the paper on the table, straightening it next to the pen. "What about me?"

"How are you doing?"

"I'm fine." Of all the people in this scenario she was the one with the least to be upset about.

"What you saw today isn't right, Sweetheart. It's okay to be bothered by it."

She huffed out a breath. "I just don't see how he can think what he does is okay. He legitimately thinks everyone else is the issue." It was the first thing Junior did when she walked in.

Started blaming her for the fact that Camille was leaving him.

"He's a narcissist."

She snorted out a half-laugh. "Not sure how that's possible. He's disgusting." Mae sighed, the weight of all she'd witnessed tonight getting heavier with each passing second, the compression making room for what-ifs to sneak in the open cracks.

"I don't know what would have happened if you weren't there tonight." She kept her eyes off Boone. Looking at him didn't seem like a good idea. "Things could have been so much worse."

"Mae."

"Hmm?" She kept her gaze on the table beside her.

"Look at me, Mae."

She swallowed, the tightness of her throat making it a difficult action.

"Please?"

It was a bad idea. She was as sure of it now as she was before. Nothing good would come from looking at Boone right now.

But not looking at him was feeling just as bad.

She slowly lifted her gaze to his. The swollen skin around his eye was barely tinted with a shade of purple that could almost be pink. Her hand lifted to the spot, fingers carefully brushing the heated line of his cheekbone. "He hurt you."

"Don't think for a second it's not worth it."

Mae let her fingers move down the shadowed skin of his cheek, over the rough scrape of the dusting of dark hair peeking out along his jawline.

Then they slid across his lips.

"Mae."

He said her name so softly, like maybe he didn't mean to say it at all. It pulled her gaze from where she touched him to rest on his.

So much was different now.

But maybe there might be some things that were still the same.

Mae looped one arm around his neck and pushed up on her toes.

She kissed him without intention. Without forethought.

Without plan or even realization.

She couldn't really remember what it was like to kiss Boone before. Even so, there was no way it was anything like this.

He immediately pulled her body against his, holding her tight as the ice pack he'd been holding hit the floor. One arm banded across her back and the other cradled her head.

Mae pressed closer.

To this man who hurt her so deeply.

Because she'd loved him so much.

Broke her apart and left her to clean up the mess.

And she had.

But there was always something missing.

Maybe because she never found all the pieces.

Boone pulled his lips from hers but he didn't move away. Didn't let her go as his eyes rested on hers.

Like he was waiting for her to say something. Explain the action.

But right now that was too complicated to work out.

So instead she kissed him again, this time winding her arms around his neck and holding him as tight as he held her.

She wanted more from him.

Not that she knew what that more was at this point.

His tongue traced the line of her lips and Mae immediately met it. He tasted faintly familiar, like a memory that teases you with hints of time and place, but no matter how hard you try it's impossible to find.

Only she knew where this memory was.

It was right in front of her.

"Boone, I—"

Suddenly the room spun. Boone's big body blocked her view of the door and the man who interrupted the questionable thing she'd just done.

Boone held her firmly in place as he tipped his head to look the officer's way.

"I need Mae to fill out her statement before you go."

"She'll do it."

Boone turned back to her as footsteps retreated down the hall. "You up to doing it now?"

"Um." Mae tucked her hair behind one ear as her brain scrambled to come back online. "Yeah. That's fine."

Boone pulled out one of the chairs around the table,

angling it her way. He waited until she sat down before sitting down in the chair beside her. "Write down everything you can remember."

Mae glanced up as Grady came in. He stood near the vending machine, awkwardly shifting from foot to foot. She lifted her brows in question.

"I gotta be here while you do that." His eyes went to Boone before coming back to her. "Make sure no one tells you what to write."

"Seriously?" She scoffed. "Whatever."

"I'm not saying I think you'd do that." Grady eased a little closer. "We're just tryin' to make sure we can make as much stick to him as possible."

"Good." Mae wrote the date and time across the top of the paper and started across the first line. She looked up at Boone. "You probably shouldn't read this."

"Hell, Mae," Grady dropped his head back. "Don't tell him that. I don't want to have to arrest him again."

"You didn't arrest me this time." Boone leaned back in his seat. "You detained me."

"Is there a difference?" Mae kept writing, using the conversation to take her attention off the recounting of events she still hadn't fully processed.

"I'm not the one at county, so yeah." Boone stood up and paced to the coffee maker in the corner, pouring out a cup before swigging it back. "But I'm thinkin' I might not be opposed to it now."

"You gotta let us handle this Boone." Grady was nearly a head shorter than Boone and a full year younger. He was also one of the best cops she knew. He didn't take shit but he was also compassionate and kind.

It was why she'd almost caved the hundredth time he asked her out.

But for some reason she could never make herself do it.

Because as good of a man as he was, Grady never felt right.

"Hell." Mae groaned as she dug the pen into the paper.

"What's wrong?" Boone stepped her way.

She scratched her signature across the bottom of the statement and shoved it Grady's way, her eyes never leaving Boone. She shoved a finger at Boone's chest as she walked past. "You're what's wrong."

CHAPTER ELEVEN

GRADY'S EYES FOLLOWED Mae as she walked out.

"Mae." Boone chased after her, following her down the hall and through the small station. "Slow down."

"No. I want to go home." She glanced his way.

Then she walked faster.

"What happened?" He kept pace with her, sticking right at her side. "Talk to me."

"Nothing happened." She shoved one hand in her purse, digging around as she raced toward the door.

Boone pushed it open to keep her from walking right through it. "Slow down, Sweetheart."

"No." She whipped her hand out of the purse, keys gripped tight. "I don't want to be here anymore."

"Then we don't have to be." Boone managed to get in front of her, stopping her in her tracks. "If you want to go home I'll take you home." He held his breath, reaching out to take the keys from her hand. "Okay?"

Mae looked to one side. "Okay."

Boone slowly eased her toward the passenger's side of the SUV. He pulled open the door. Mae immediately sat down. She stared out the windshield a second before looking up at him. "Have you thought about what might have happened if we didn't go to Camille's tonight?"

He had. "No, and you shouldn't either."

"But—"

He shook his head. "Thinkin' about that isn't going to do anyone any favors."

It certainly wasn't helping him any.

Boone closed the door and climbed into the driver's seat, reaching to the side of the seat and pressing the button to take it back as far as it could go.

"You're messing everything up." Mae's head fell to the headrest.

"I'll put the seat back when I get out."

"I'm not talking about the seat, Boone." Her head rolled his way. "Why couldn't you just stay gone?"

He started the SUV, buying a little time to decide how much more of the truth to give her. She deserved it all.

But all of it might be too much for her right now.

"I was never as happy gone as I was here." Hopefully that would be enough to placate her.

"Then why'd you leave?"

"I left because I was young." He risked a glance her way. "And stupid."

"I thought it was your dream to be a cowboy?" It was a simple question instead of the accusation he expected from her.

"So did I." He thought it would be impossible to explain

what happened to Mae, but now that he was facing it down, the words were surprisingly simple. "I was wrong."

"Huh." Mae turned to look out the side window. "You think he'll come back to try to hurt Camille?"

"It would not be in Junior's best interest to try to get close to Camille again." He'd called Brooks the second he could, intending to send his brother out to make sure Mae and Camille were okay.

Turned out Brooks already knew where they were.

"I thought Bill was going to lose his shit." Mae turned back his way. "Your mom had to work hard to calm him down."'

"There's only a handful of things my dad gets worked up about. That's one of them."

"What are the rest?"

Boone smiled. "Taxes and someone else eating the last piece of pie."

"That's because your mom makes good pie."

"Not as good as you." He turned his smile on Mae.

"You've never had my pie."

"My source is reliable." Boone pulled into the lot at the back of The Wooden Spoon and parked her car next to his. He reached into his pocket and pulled out the keys to his truck.

Mae didn't make a move to get out. Her lips pursed, shifting to one side, then the other. She ran her fingernail over a loose thread on her purse. "I might have a little pie on hand now."

He'd watched her pull the line of them from the ovens before they left for Camille's and if his nose hadn't betrayed him, he might even know what kind they were. "If you're sure you have some to spare."

"I mean, it's my most popular kind, so there's not really spare." Her eyes finally came his way. "It would be more like you getting in at the front of the line."

"I'm flattered."

"You should be." Mae almost smiled. "There's a lot of people who'd knock you down to take your place."

"There's a lot of *men* who would knock me down, and it's got nothing to do with your pie." He let his smile slide to one side. "Not in the technical sense anyway."

"If you make a joke about eating my pie then my offer's off the table."

"What if it's not a joke?"

She slung her purse at him before opening her door and climbing out into the dimming light of the lot.

Brody jumped out too. "I take it back." He laughed as she rolled her eyes his way, the line of her mouth teasing a smile. "I promise not to say anything else about your pie."

"I don't believe you."

"You probably shouldn't." He leaned against the building as she unlocked the deadbolt. "I promise not to say anything else about your pie today."

Mae lifted a brow as she pulled the door open.

"I promise not to say anything about your pie for the next five minutes."

"That sounds like a stretch." Mae walked into the kitchen of The Wooden Spoon, dropping her purse onto the counter just inside the door. "But I appreciate that you're trying not to make promises you can't keep."

It was a dig. One that he felt.

"I'm not the same as I was, Mae. I'm tryin' to show you that."

Mae turned toward him, one of the pies in her hands. "I'm not the same either, Boone." She set the dessert on the counter between them. "So where does that leave us?"

"At the beginning."

It was what he'd realized they had to have. A fresh start. They were both different people with different lives. There was no way to pick up where they left off.

The people who left off didn't exist anymore.

Mae shook her head. "I can't pretend like the past didn't happen." Her eyes dipped to where she ran a small knife through the upper crust of the pie. She lifted the first piece out, sliding it onto a small plate before pushing it his way.

He stared down at it. "This is peach pie, Mae."

She didn't respond as she cut the next slice free.

Mae could say she hated him.

She could say there was no way for them to start over.

But that single slice of pie said different.

"I make all sorts of pies." Mae tried to brush it off.

Boone picked up the plate and cut off a chunk with the edge of his fork. He knew what it would be even before the first burst of ginger hit his tongue.

Mae tapped her fingers on the counter, her eyes going anywhere but his way.

This was a version of a pie he knew well. One he hadn't had in years.

His mother made it for him growing up. Ginger peach pie replaced his birthday cakes from the time he was a kid until he left Moss Creek.

Boone set the plate on the stainless-steel counter,

dropping it harder than he meant to, sending the fork rattling off the ceramic and onto the steel.

Mae thought of him.

Found a way to take his favorite pie and make it even better.

Maybe she did it to prove how wrong he was to leave her behind.

She was right.

Maybe she did it to prove she was better than he should ever have.

She was right on that too.

Whatever it was, Mae thought of him like he thought of her.

Still kept a piece of him in her life.

He rounded the counter as the fork continued bouncing around, tipping over the edge and clattering to the floor.

Mae's eyes lifted to his just as he reached for her, holding her face in his hands.

"It's just pie." She tried one more time to convince him of the lie.

But the whisper of her words made it clear she didn't even believe it herself.

It wasn't just pie any more than she was just some girl he used to love.

Her hands were in his shirt, gripping the fabric tight as he pulled her close. Boone let his lips hover just over hers.

He took a breath, pulling the scent of her skin into his lungs. Even after a full day of work in the kitchen she still smelled sweet and soft.

And faintly of the peach pie filling that still lingered on his tongue.

Her eyes opened, holding his as he slowly closed the tiny gap remaining between them.

Her lips were so soft.

Full and warm against his. So much of her was different, but this was exactly as he remembered.

Boone pulled her closer, dropping his hands from her face to her neck. Her shoulders.

Her back.

Mae pushed into him as her hands moved over his chest to grip his shoulders. The friction of her body against his was something no part of him could ignore.

Since the night he saw her in that soaking wet dress he'd imagined all those soft curves pressed into him.

What they would feel like.

What they would look like.

He left a girl and came home to a woman. One who knew her worth. Knew her strength.

One who was comfortable with who she was.

And what she wanted.

Mae's hands slid down his body, the tips of her fingers digging into his skin through the fabric of his shirt. Nothing about her touch was hesitant or bashful.

Each slide of her tongue was confident. A little assertive.

She grabbed his shirt, pulling it free of his jeans. Then her hands were on his bare skin, moving over his stomach and across his pecs.

Boone gripped her waist, picking her up and setting her butt on the counter. It freed up his hands and brought her to his height.

It also aligned her body to his, a fact Mae immediately capitalized on. Her legs wrapped around his waist, pulling his aching dick tight to her body in a move that pulled a groan from his chest. Her hands went to his head, knocking his hat to the floor as her fingers forked into his hair, gripping it tight as she sucked his lower lip between her teeth.

Boone palmed a soft hip with one hand and her chin with the other, holding her in place as he put some space between them.

Gave himself some room to think.

To breathe.

"What's wrong?" The sly twist of her lips made it clear Mae knew exactly what was wrong.

"I'm just tryin' to wrap my head around what's happening."

Her eyes skimmed down his front. "If you don't know what's happening then I might rethink inviting you upstairs."

"I'm not coming upstairs, Mae. Not tonight."

She scoffed. "What? I thought this was what you wanted."

"This is the least of what I want where you're concerned." He shoved her butt farther back on the counter, trying to find any extra space he could.

"You don't want to fuck me?"

"Jesus." He raked one hand through his hair. "I'm going to need you to not say shit like that right now."

"I can say whatever I want. It's not my problem if you're not man enough to handle me." She shoved at his chest, knocking him back before jumping down and storming toward the stairs leading to her apartment.

Boone caught her before she hit the first step, snagging

one hand and spinning her to face him as he backed her against the bit of wall between the back door and the stairwell. "Is that what you think, Mae? That I'm not man enough to handle you?"

She held his gaze, lips pressed together.

He leaned down, evening his eyes with hers. "If you want to torture me then that's fine. Say it again. I'll stand here and take it like the fucking man I am." He eased in a little more. "But don't think for a second that I won't give back as much as I take when the time comes, Sweetheart."

He hadn't really considered the effect the statement might have on her or he wouldn't have said it.

But it was too late now.

A hint of pink spread over her neck and her pupils dilated. The full lips that were just under his parted, teasing him with a soft gasp.

But that wasn't the worst Mae had to dish out.

The tip of her tongue skimmed across those parted lips. Her eyes locked onto his. "Why don't you want to fuck me, Boone?"

"It's not about lack of want, Sweetheart." He pressed into her a little more. If he was going to suffer then he was sure as hell going to make sure he wasn't the only one.

Only difference was, he'd put her out of her misery.

"It's about knowing when the time's right." Boone shifted, sliding one of his legs between hers, pressing his thigh tight to her body. "And the time is not right." He flexed the hand at her hip, testing the softness there. He wanted to memorize every bit of her. Every curve. Every dip.

Every breath.

"Maybe this is your only shot."

"If this is my only shot then the time's definitely not right." Boone leaned into her neck, running his lips over the soft skin there. "Because I don't plan for it to be a one-time deal when I take you to my bed." He nipped at the spot where her shoulder met her neck. "When I take you to my bed I plan to keep you there."

Mae whimpered a little as he put more pressure between her legs. "What about my bed?"

"The bed isn't the issue, Sweetheart." He skimmed his fingers up her side. "The issue is I came home with the intention of making you mine again, and I can promise you that once I fuck you I won't be letting you go again."

Mae pushed into him, finding a little friction where his leg held her pinned in place. "I like when you say that word." Her head tipped to one side as he teased the spot under her ear with his teeth and tongue.

"I think you might just be a handful, Mae Wells." He teased the underside of her breast, skimming his fingers along the fullness tempting him to take this a little further.

"You might be surprised what I am."

"I look forward to it." Boone traced up the swell, running the flats of his fingers over the tip, groaning a little when it hardened almost immediately. "Hopefully I can surprise you too." He teased the tight bud, pinching it through the fabric of her shirt.

"Hopefully." The word was a little breathy. A little husky.

And it was making him crazy as hell.

He needed to walk away. Kiss Mae goodnight and take himself home for a cold shower and a minute to think about everything that happened today.

But he didn't want to leave her. Not like this.

He wanted to leave her with something to think about.
Motivation to spend time with him again.
He wanted her to see him for what he could be.
The one to take care of her needs.
All of them.

CHAPTER TWELVE

HER BODY WAS on fire.

Every freaking inch of it.

Skin.

Lungs.

And most definitely her brain. It was the part responsible for inviting Boone into her bed.

Which he promptly rejected.

And that only made the flames taking her over burn hotter.

There was no way to compare this man to the one she knew before him. They looked the same. Sounded the same. Shared the same name.

But the man with her now was different. Different enough to cut through everything she put between them.

It wasn't easy. It wasn't fast.

But he stuck with it, fighting in spite of all that was in front of him.

That might be the most important part.

Boone's thumb worked across her nipple with a

maddeningly slow stroke, teasing it with a pinch that was just barely too-little. She arched into his touch, trying to get more from him.

As much as he would give her.

The leg between her thighs was exactly the same. A tease that gave her just enough to make her crazy.

Mae rubbed against it, stealing a little more sensation. A little more friction.

Boone growled low in his chest as his body rocked against hers. The hand on her breast moved away, making her huff out a sharp breath in protest.

"Relax, Sweetheart." Boone's fingers gripped her shirt, dragging it up. His touch brushed her bare belly, warm palm flattening against her exposed skin.

Sliding up.

Her heart raced as the anticipation built.

She'd been with Boone before. Done this same exact thing with him more times than she could count.

But it still felt completely new.

His touch was steadier. Slower.

Focused.

Filled with intent and purpose.

His hand eased up, taking her pulse with it. When it slid to her back she scoffed in frustration.

Boone chuckled low and deep as his fingers worked the clasp of her bra. "I don't remember you being so impatient."

"I don't remember you being so slow."

Boone's head lifted, his blue eyes settling on hers. "If you think I'm rushing anything I do with you or to you, then you should probably pull up a chair and get comfortable, because I intend to enjoy every fucking second of you."

Good Lord.

Maybe Boone's refusal to take her to bed was a good thing, because right this second she was about to pass out.

His lips curved into a slow smile that made the heat licking through her body surge up like someone threw gasoline on it. "That's what I thought." Boone's hand trailed around her ribs, back to front, before teasing along the lower line of her breast. "We're taking baby steps, Sweetheart." His head dipped, mouth coming to slide over hers with a barely-there touch. "Because I need to make sure you understand what you're getting yourself into here."

She was willing to get into anything he wanted her to at this point.

Every second that passed. Every move he made. Every word he said, made the truth of the situation more and more clear.

This Boone might be different. He might be someone she didn't really know like she thought she did.

But there was one thing about him that was very much the same.

Boone didn't half-ass anything. It's what led to the offer that took him from Moss Creek.

From her.

And so she'd hated that about him. The way he worked doggedly to be the best he was capable of being.

Now?

Now maybe it would finally work in her favor.

"I'm in Moss Creek for one reason, and one reason only, Mae." He kept talking, but the words were simply background noise because most of her attention was fixed on where his fingers worked higher, under the loosened lace of her bra. "I came back for you." He caught her nipple between his finger and thumb, finally giving her what she'd been so desperate to have. "I came back to make you mine again."

What he was saying was too much to process.

To consider.

Luckily he was giving her plenty more to focus on.

His lips were on her neck as he spoke, moving to her collar bone as her shirt lifted more, bra and all pushing higher until the cool air reached her already tight nipples. When the heat of his mouth closed around one her head fell against the wall at her back. His teeth and tongue stroked and raked in a steady rhythm that shot straight to where his thigh pressed to her throbbing pussy. "Boone."

He growled again, the rumble adding an extra level of stimulation to where his lips were locked on her nipple.

His mouth pulled free, holding the suction until the last possible second as it dragged off her. It immediately came to hers, taking full ownership of a kiss that stole what little breath she'd managed to maintain.

"I want to touch you." His lips didn't leave hers as he spoke. One hand went to the button of her pants and stopped. "Mae. Open your eyes."

Her lids were heavy as she fought them up. His eyes were on her, strong and steady.

"Can I touch you?"

"Yes." It rushed out. Hopefully he would rush too.

But like he promised, Boone was in no hurry. One finger dipped into the waistband of her jeans, hooking and using the grip to pull her against him.

Mae gripped his dark hair as he kissed her again. He shifted, stealing the thigh that was keeping her from losing her mind. One hand gripped her leg, lifting it up and hooking it around his hip. He ground against her, the rigid line of his dick making it clear she was not the only one enjoying the interaction.

Finally his thumb flipped the button of her pants open. He dragged the zipper down, each rake of the teeth making her stomach clench tighter with anticipation.

When his hand tucked into her panties her breathing stalled, every nerve in her body waiting for that first touch.

When he brushed her clit she nearly fell. Probably would have if Boone hadn't been holding her up.

When he didn't immediately get to work where she wanted him Mae tried to press into his hand.

"Uh-uh." Boone's hand went to her hip, gripping it tight, holding her in place. "You're not taking this from me, Sweetheart."

She wanted to rage at him for teasing her. Wanted to scream. Yell at him to get on with it.

But the sound that came out of her could best be described as a whimper. A needy mewl.

She worked hard not to need anything from anyone. Ever.

All because of him.

Now he was turning that on its head. It was one more thing she couldn't dwell on. Not right now.

Probably not tomorrow either.

His touch was steady and slow, easing over her slick skin, stroking just enough to get her almost where she wanted to go.

But not quite.

"Please." Her head fell forward, resting against his shoulder as he made another pass that fell just short.

"I'm not always going to give you what you want, Sweetheart." Boone's fingers eased inside her, dragging over a spot that she felt deep in her core. His thumb rested on her clit. "But I promise I will always give you what you deserve." He moved over the two spots in some sort of coordinated effort that narrowed her vision and muffled all the sounds around her.

Focused every sense on that divinely perfect motion that made every second leading up to this worth it.

Her whole body went tight and time stopped. The world was black and silent for a heartbeat.

Then it shattered apart.

And she shattered along with it.

Only one thing held her together.

The same man who once broke her.

No. Not the same man.

The new man here in his place.

Boone's lips never left her skin as she waited for the room to stop spinning. His hands held her tight. His body held her up.

Anchoring her while everything shifted around her.

And it was only partly due to whatever he'd just done to her.

By the time she was able to string two thoughts together, Boone was fastening her jeans.

Her bra was back in place and hooked tight.

Her shirt was righted.

Everything he'd upended was back where it belonged.

Almost everything.

"You need to go to bed." Boone's body was still against hers. Still there, solid and strong.

"Okay."

He kissed her one final time, his lips moving across her jaw to rest at her ear. "Goodnight, Mae." His body eased off hers.

She was stuck in place as he backed to the door, pulling it open and slipping out. Before it closed his deep voice carried through the gap. "I'm not leaving until I hear this lock."

"Okay." Mae managed to move her feet to the door as it clicked shut. She twisted the deadbolt then leaned against it, resting her forehead on the cool steel.

She closed her eyes, listening to the sound of the engine as Boone started his truck and pulled out of the lot.

And for the first time in her life she was glad he left.

———

"THAT'S HOT."

"It's a fucking train wreck, that's what it is." Mae sat across from Liza, her closest and best friend. She huffed out a sigh as she stabbed her fork into the lunch she'd dished up for them. Their normal lunch day was Thursday, but after last night it became clear she needed an intervention and she needed it now. "What in the hell am I going to do?"

"For starters you're going to let him do that to you again." Liza shoved in a bite of shrimp salad, shaking her head. "I wish someone would do that to me."

"Really?" Mae glanced out at the tables lined with young, virile ranch hands. "I'm pretty sure we can find enough volunteers to keep you busy for the next three weeks."

"I can't screw around with one of my ranch hands." Liza huffed out a breath. "Talk about a train wreck."

"Then pick from one of the other ranches." Mae smiled. "There's plenty to go around."

"Meh." Liza glanced up as the kitchen door swung open. "Where's Camille? I haven't seen her yet today."

Mae tried to keep her reaction neutral. "Camille just accepted a new job."

Liza's brows lifted. "Really?"

"Maryann Pace offered her the general manager position at The Inn."

Liza's expression hardened. "I'm sure Junior'll love that."

"I'm sure it will be fine." It was only a matter of time before Liza found out what happened, but right now Mae didn't have it in her to be the one to tell her. "How's everything going at the ranch?" Mae steered the conversation to more comfortable territory.

"Good enough." Liza shrugged her shoulders. "The bills are paid and no one's walked off the job in a while so I'm gonna call it a win."

Liza was one of the few female ranch owners around, and her gender alone probably wouldn't have been an issue if she'd come into it a different sort of way.

But the circumstances around her ownership of Cross Creek Ranch were unfortunate and still speculated on by people who liked to talk out their asses.

"Ben seems to have everything under control." The lead hand at Cross Creek came into The Wooden Spoon at least once a week, usually with a few other men in tow.

"Ben's a good guy."

"Good-looking too." Mae wiggled her brows at Liza.

"He's single." Liza smirked around her straw. "You could always ditch Boone like he ditched you and go after Ben."

Mae's stomach turned, twisting around the load of shrimp salad she'd whipped up right before Liza got there. "There's nothing to ditch. It's not like he and I are anything."

"I'm gonna go out on a limb and say any man who services a woman without expecting to get his own rocks off is probably a man who's looking for more than a fuck buddy."

Mae opened her eyes wide at the silver head sitting right behind Liza. She leaned in. "You're going to give Mrs. Tucker a heart attack."

Liza waved her off. "If you think Mrs. Tucker doesn't know exactly what I'm talking about then you've never heard the stories about how Mr. Tucker convinced her to marry him."

Mae leaned a little to one side, peeking at Mr. Tucker's lined face. The old couple came in three times a week, Monday, Wednesday, and Friday for an early supper. They held hands across the table every single time. She straightened. "How have you heard these stories?"

Liza shrugged. "She tells me one every time I see her." She smiled. "People seem to want to tell me things."

She wasn't wrong. "That's why I don't like to shop with you. We always end up hearing way too much information about whoever's running the register."

Liza's eyes went wide. "Did I tell you that Marsha at the Dollar General caught her husband cheating on her?"

"Doesn't surprise me. He's a twat." One of the perks of running the main eatery in town meant everyone came there.

It was also one of the downfalls.

Liza eyed Mae. "Damn it, Mae. How am I supposed to know which lines to avoid if you don't tell me what's going on in town?"

"In case you haven't noticed, I'm a little busy. I don't have time to keep you abreast of all the town scandal." Mae smiled a little when her friend scoffed.

"Then what is this friendship going to be built on? Mutual respect and compatible senses of humor?"

"That does seem pretty flimsy now that I'm thinking about it." Liza was one of the few people in town she could really be herself with. It had been that way from day one. Maybe it was because Liza didn't know her when she was young, like most people in town did.

It meant Liza didn't expect her to be what she used to be.

Liza let out a breath as she leaned back in her seat. "I should get going. I need to run to the bank and the post office while I'm in town." She started stacking their plates and flatware. "You need anything while I'm running around?"

"Nah. I'm good." Mae stopped telling Liza she didn't have to clean up the mess after their third lunch together. "You get any better at bussing and I'm going to offer you a job." Mae managed to snag their glasses as Liza balanced the rest on her palms.

"I didn't even think about that." Liza scooted out of her seat. "Camille working at The Inn means she won't be working here with you anymore."

"Guess that means you should come work with me then." Mae shot Liza a grin. "Because I'm sure you don't have enough on your plate to deal with."

Liza groaned. "Who knew it was so much work to wrangle a ranch full of men." She shook her head as they made their way into the kitchen. "They're more dramatic than any woman I've ever met."

Mae snorted out a laugh. "All I can picture is a bunch of cowboys dramatically draping themselves across hay bales."

"Their drama is less about draping and more about fighting." Liza set their plates in the sink where Boone stood not so long ago. "I swear one of them always has a black eye."

"Turn the hose on them." A deep voice sent Mae and Liza spinning toward the back door of the kitchen.

Mae's heart skipped a beat at the sight of him. Last night Boone made no promises or plans about when he wanted to see her again.

A tiny part of her wanted to dig into that fact, hold it tight as a reminder of what he'd done.

Boone's eyes lingered on Mae a second before moving to Liza. "That's what my mom does when things get outta hand."

"If it's good enough for Maryann Pace then it's good enough for me." Liza gave Boone a grin and a wink. "I gotta get going." She turned toward Mae as she walked past, wiggling her brows. "Have a nice afternoon."

Boone stepped in close to Mae's side, one hand coming to rest on the small of her back. "She definitely will."

CHAPTER THIRTEEN

HE'D PLANNED TO wait for Mae to come to him.

But the lure of being close to her was too strong to resist.

"What are you doing here?" It wasn't the accusation it was the last time she asked.

"I was in town and thought I'd stop by to see if you had any plans for the afternoon." It was a fib.

He had come to town, but it was with the sole intention of coming to see her.

"You mean after I bake fifteen pies?" Mae's lips hinted at a smile.

"Only fifteen?" Boone followed her to the same spot where she'd worked the day before to assemble the peach pie that told him what she never would have.

"I'm trying a new recipe and I'm not sure how popular it will be." Mae reached under the counter to a small refrigerator. She pulled out a large container of yellowish liquid. "Sometimes they love new things, sometimes they leave them and then I'm stuck with ten pies."

"I'll buy any you have leftover. My mother would love it."

"Trying to get back in her good graces?" Mae reached up to pull down a crust-lined pie pan.

"There's only one woman's good graces I'm worried about." Boone relaxed against the counter as Mae carefully poured some of the liquid over the crumb-style crust.

"Mm-hmm." She ducked her head, but didn't manage to hide the smile trying to work across her mouth.

"So what's this new pie you're trying?" Boone glanced around the kitchen as the staff worked together, cleaning up the mess of the day while the waitresses cleared out the dining room. It was clear Mae was good at more than just cooking. Her business ran like a well-oiled machine, and that was due to one person and her impeccable leadership.

"It's called Carolina Beach Pie." Mae moved on to the next pie pan. "It's a salty cracker crust with a lemon custard filling." She moved down the line, filling the pans one by one with a careful and steady pour. "After you bake it you chill it and top it with whipped cream."

"So a salty sweet sort of thing."

"Salty, sweet, and sour." She did smile now. "All the best things in one pie."

"Sounds like I'm not getting any." He was only mildly disappointed at the fact. "'Cause you're going to sell out early."

"We'll see." She lifted the first one and turned toward the ovens.

Boone grabbed the next and followed behind her, setting it down as she slid the first one into the oven. He went back for the next one, bringing it just as she grabbed the previous one. It continued like that, him bringing them over, Mae loading them into the heat, until all the pies were baking.

"How long do they bake?"

"Only about fifteen minutes." Mae set one of the many timers placed around the kitchen. "That's one of the reasons I hope it sells well. It takes a lot less time to prepare."

"Bein' too popular isn't always a good problem to have I guess."

Mae lifted one shoulder. "There's only so much of me to go around."

"And no one wants to spend their whole life working."

Mae tapped one finger on the counter. "I guess that depends on what else you have to do."

"What *does* a woman like you do with her free time?" He'd wanted to come here and surprise her with an afternoon she would enjoy, unfortunately it was entirely possible he had no clue what Mae liked to do anymore.

Mae rocked on her feet a little. "I mostly just work."

"If I remember correctly, you were on a date not too long ago." One that clearly had not gone well since he hadn't seen hide nor hair of the bastard sniffing around town.

The man clearly didn't know what he was missing out on.

"Um." Mae's eyes dropped to the floor. "He actually canceled that night."

She'd been coming back from Billings. She was dressed up. Even soaked to the skin it was clear she'd done her hair and makeup that night. "When did this cancellation happen?"

Mae shook her head, eyes still avoiding his. "I was already at the restaurant."

"What a dumbass." Boone edged in closer. "Not that I'm not appreciative of his dumbassery."

153

Mae crossed her arms. "He was actually really smart."

"Smart and dumbass aren't mutually exclusive." Boone leaned in, resting his hands on the edge of the counter at each side of her hips. "What restaurant did you go to?"

"Thomasino's."

"Did you pick it or did he?"

"I did." Mae gave him a sly smile. "If I'm going to eat at a restaurant that I don't own, I sure as hell want it to be a good one."

"Smart woman." Boone studied her for a minute. "What about hiking? You used to love that."

"I haven't been hiking in years."

"Why not?"

Mae shrugged. "No time."

"What about now?"

Her grey eyes drifted to the ovens behind him. "Well, I'm currently baking fifteen pies, so..."

"They're going to be done soon." Boone lifted his head, making a show of looking around the empty space. "And everyone else seems to be gone for the day."

Mae's eyes skimmed down his t-shirt. She snagged the fabric over his stomach and wiggled it from side to side. "That why you're dressed like this? Because you think I'll go for a hike with you?"

"I don't always dress like a cowboy, Sweetheart."

"You used to."

"That was back when I thought that was what I wanted to be when I grew up." Boone spent so much of his life thinking that would be all he'd ever want. To travel the country doing what he'd worked so hard at.

Fame. Money. Excitement. It had all of it.

But it wasn't enough.

Not nearly.

"You *were* a cowboy when you grew up." Mae dropped his shirt, her arms wrapping back across her chest, making a barrier between them.

He knew this would be a one step forward, two steps back sort of thing, but it was hard not to want to pick up right where they left off last night.

But this was for Mae. All of it had to be. He'd gotten what he thought he wanted. Now it was her turn.

Hopefully she made a better choice than he did.

"I might argue that I'm not so sure I grew up when I thought I did." Boone reached out to brush back a bit of sandy hair. "Takes some of us a lot longer to be the men we look like on the outside."

Mae's eyes slid down his front and her lower lip slowly edged between her teeth.

Last night was a rude awakening for him. He'd expected Mae to be more experienced.

He just didn't expect her to be able to bring him to his knees.

And she'd come close.

Which meant he had to tread lightly. Make sure he proved just what he could do before she took him down.

The timer started to whine, stopping him from hearing whatever she might have said next.

Mae scooted away from him, going to the first pie. "I guess we have some time while these cool before I can put them in the cooler." Her eyes came his way for a second. "It might be nice to get outside."

"It might." Boone stayed out of her way since there

wasn't much he could do to help at this point.

Once all the pies were lined down the counter to cool, Mae untied the apron covering her front and pulled it over her head before tossing it into a basket in the corner. "I'm going to take a quick shower and change so we don't get eaten by a bear who thinks I'm pie." She walked to the stairs, pausing to turn his way. "You can come up."

Another step. One he'd probably lose soon enough, but he was still taking it.

Mae was already headed up the steps when he hit the bottom. Looking up at the curve of her ass as she ran up the stairs wasn't going to help his cause any, but it was another opportunity he couldn't make himself pass on.

"Stop looking at my ass." Mae peeked at him over one shoulder.

"Yes, ma'am."

She laughed. It was light and easy as it echoed through the well around them. "So polite."

"I try to be a gentleman when I can." He reached the landing as she unlocked the door. It opened into a small utility room with a washer and dryer along with other necessities like a water heater and furnace. Just outside the utility room door the space completely opened up. The ceilings were high and the windows were tall. It was one big open area that made up a living room, dining room, and kitchen. "Holy hell, Mae."

"It's nice, isn't it?"

"Nice doesn't do it justice." Thick crown molding edged the ceilings. The trim around the original windows and floors was solid wood, stained a rich mahogany color. "This place is beautiful."

Mae gave him a soft smile. "Thanks." She thumbed over one shoulder. "I'm going to go get ready." She didn't move. Her eyes stayed on him as she rubbed her lips together. Finally she backed toward the door behind her. "I'll be right back."

He knew it might be a little awkward between them today. Things changed last night. It would take her some time to adjust.

Because Mae wasn't where he was yet, and she might not be for a while.

Boone went to the front windows that looked out over Main Street. The blinds were pulled open, letting the early evening sun pour into the space.

How many times had he looked up at these same windows? How many times had he wondered if he'd ever be on the other side of them?

Hundreds.

"It's strange to look down on it, isn't it?" Mae stepped in at his side, her eyes moving over the town below them. "I remember the first time I stood here. Everything looked so different."

He tipped his head to watch her. "Everything was different."

"Maybe." She reached up to pull the cord, lowering the blinds before walking to the fridge in the open kitchen. "You want a bottle of water?"

"Sure." Boone waited for her to collect her keys and the water before following Mae back down the stairs and out into the lot where his truck was parked next to hers. She lifted her eyes his way, raising a brow along with them.

"I practically work here now." He went to open her door.

"I provide the owner with certain services." Mae's skin immediately flushed and it made him want to push his luck. "At her convenience, of course."

"I'm not sure anything about you is convenient." Mae reached out to grab the handle of the door and pulled it closed, leaving him laughing alone in the lot.

She smothered a smile from her spot in his truck, tipping back one of the bottles of water as he hurried to the driver's door. He climbed in beside her and started the engine. "You want the air conditioning or you want the windows down?"

"Still windows down." Mae pressed the button on her door, lowering her window and letting in the warm spring air.

"What else hasn't changed?" Boone rolled his own window down and rested his arm across the opening.

"I still hate liver." She relaxed back in her seat as the wind whipped around the cab, loosening a few hairs from her fresh braid. "Still love trash television." Mae was quiet for a minute. "What about you?"

"Well," his brain stalled out. He'd been so focused on showing how he was different that he hadn't really considered how he might still be the same. "I still like peach pie."

Mae smiled.

"I still wear boxers."

"You know my momma found a pair of your underwear in my room once. She almost died."

"I remember the night I lost those." He'd climbed out her window when her parents came home early from a dinner party. "I was pretty sure I might die that night." Boone glanced at Mae. "It would have been worth it."

"Maybe."

His head snapped her way.

Mae laughed, loud and long, head back, eyes closed.

"You know, you keep on I'm gonna have a hell of a lot to prove."

Mae turned to look him dead in the eye. "What makes you think I didn't already know that?"

"Hell." He turned to face the windshield.

"Having second thoughts, Cowboy?"

"About you?" He reached across the console to snag her hand. "Never."

"You mean never again."

He laced his fingers between hers. "I've never had a second thought about you, Mae." He pulled into the small parking area of one of the county-owned parks. "You were never what I second guessed. I was what I second guessed."

How could he explain what it had taken him years to realize?

The fear that really fueled his decision to leave Moss Creek.

To leave Mae.

"That's not what it felt like."

"And that's on me." He ran his thumb over her soft skin. "And it's on me to make up for it."

"I'm not sure you can." The truth in her words hit him hard even though he should have expected it.

Like getting bucked off an unbroken horse.

"That's okay." He held her hand tighter, needing the reminder that she was at least giving him the chance to try.

Her gaze was a weight as it rested on the side of his face.

One he felt. One he would gladly carry every day for the rest of his life if she'd let him.

Boone parked the truck, wishing he didn't have to let her hand go to switch the engine off. "Ready?"

"I guess I have to be." Mae opened her door and slid to the ground, taking both water bottles with her.

He reached into the back and pulled out the backpack he'd loaded with a few things, hoping Mae would agree to come out with him. Mae was standing at the trailhead, looking over the map by the time he got to her side. "Here." He took the bottles from her and slid them into the insulated portion of the pack.

Mae lifted a brow. "Looks like you came prepared."

"I like to be optimistic." He zipped the back and pulled it onto his shoulders. "Which trail do you want to take?"

Mae's eyes slid back to the map. "I haven't been here in years. I don't even know."

He pointed to his favorite of the trails. "This one here is the longest, but it has the best views."

Mae's gaze slid his way. "You remember the trails here?"

"I would hope so. I was just here last week." He took her hand again, leading her to the trail he walked when the weight of his bad decisions bogged him down.

"Really." Mae let him pull her along. "You hike."

"I do."

"If I remember correctly, I used to have to practically drag you hiking."

"Maybe I've learned a few things in the past ten years." He glanced down at her, the urge to remind her how different he was across the board strong. "Besides what I showed you last night."

CHAPTER FOURTEEN

SHE ALMOST MISSED a step.

Almost fell on her face over just the mention of what else Boone might have learned while he was off traveling the country.

And apparently hiking.

His hand tightened around hers. "You okay?"

She heard the smile in his voice.

"I stepped on a rock." It was a bold-faced lie that she would repeat until the day she died.

"We might have to go boot shopping if you decide to like hiking again."

"I never stopped liking to hike." Mae stepped over a branch. "I just didn't have the time."

Or anyone to go with.

Liza worked almost around the clock. Camille had a whole slew of shit to deal with. Clara had a fiancé and three kiddos to wrangle.

"I thought The Wooden Spoon closed at three."

"It does, but for a long time I ran with a really small

staff and I picked up the slack." Mae took a deep breath. The air around them smelled like pine and fresh earth. It brought an odd sense of peace she hadn't felt in a long time.

So she took another.

"It's nice out here, isn't it?"

"It is." She'd spent most of her time inside since deciding to go to culinary school a few months after Boone left. "I forgot how good it smells."

"It's nothing compared to how the kitchen at The Wooden Spoon smells, but it's a decent second." Boone lifted a branch cutting across their path, holding it out of the way as she passed under it.

"Doesn't seem like many people take this trail." The trail under their feet was starting to narrow.

"It's not an easy one." Boone moved in front of her as the foliage started to close in around them, making it impossible to walk side-by-side. His hand stayed in hers, keeping her close and providing support as the terrain got steeper. "But the view at the end is worth it."

"It better be or you don't get any Carolina Beach pie."

He laughed. "Is that how you're planning to keep me in line? Threats of pie withholding?"

"It's a pretty good plan."

"It's actually a very good plan." Boone pulled her a little closer with the hand holding hers. "You'd be shocked at the things I would do to have a taste of your pie."

Mae groaned. "I thought you were trying to prove what a grown-up man you were?"

"Pie jokes are funny no matter how old you are."

"I think we're on completely different pages on that one."

Mae skidded a little on the loose dirt. She grabbed onto Boone's shirt for balance as they scaled a steep incline.

"You want to be in the front?"

"I'm not sure that will make much of a difference." She'd put on the sneakers she wore when she wasn't working and they clearly didn't have enough tread to offer the amount of traction this trail required. A yelp jumped out as her feet once again slid out from under her.

Boone turned just in time to catch her as she went down. His hands held her steady as she struggled to find some footing.

"Here." He slid the pack off his back. "Put this on."

"Is this so I can just roll on my back and ride it down the hill?" She held onto a nearby tree as Boone tightened the straps, snugging them up to her shoulders.

Then he turned around and crouched down, pressing his back to her belly as he gripped her thighs and hefted her up off the ground.

This time her yelp was more of a loud screech. Mae wrapped both arms around his shoulders. "What are you doing?"

"I'm trying to convince you to come hiking with me and I'm pretty sure that won't happen if you bust your sweet little ass." He bounced her body, bringing it up a little higher on his back.

"Now you're going to bust both our asses." Mae tucked her head close to his as they went under a low-hanging branch.

"If we go down we go down together, Sweetheart."

"I'm going to vote that we don't go down at all." She did her best to hang onto him tight enough to alleviate some of the strain her added weight must be causing. "I definitely can't work like I do with a broken leg."

"There would be a mutiny if you couldn't work." Boone straightened as the terrain evened out a little. "They'd string me up in the center of town."

"I'm not sure it would be that bad."

"You're right." He tipped his head back to grin at her. "It would probably be worse." Boone leaned to one side to dodge a wayward limb. "And I wouldn't blame them. You've done a hell of a job with it."

She smiled. "Thank you."

"What's next?"

"What do you mean?"

"You've conquered the culinary world. What now?"

She snorted. "I'd hardly call running a diner in a tiny town conquering the culinary world." Mae sighed. "I don't know what's next. I feel like I just now can catch my breath."

"Then maybe you just take some time to breathe. Figure out where to go from here." Boone slowed in front of a thicker patch of trees. "I'm gonna put you down now."

Mae slid down his back, being careful not to choke him as she went down. "Is the rest flat?"

"This is it." Boone pushed into the thick brush. He paused, turning to look her way. "You coming?"

"Am I gonna get ticks?"

"Maybe. Sometimes you have to suffer for the good stuff." He winked. "I promise to check you over real good later if you want me to."

"Is this because I made you stop with the pie jokes?"

"Definitely." Boone backed into the thicket. "Come on. You know you want to."

Mae huffed out a breath as she followed him into what turned out to be a pretty narrow pack of trees and brush. In just a few of Boone's long steps he was breaking through the other side.

He stood at the edge, holding the last of the greenery up and out of her way.

The second she stepped out her breath caught. "I've never been to this part of the park before."

Moss Creek sat near the edge of the mountains, but most of the area out near Cross Creek and Red Cedar was flat and even. The park they were at was at the opposite edge of town and the difference in elevation was more than she'd realized. "How did we get up this high?"

"We drove part of it and I carried you up the rest." Boone wrapped one arm around her, resting his hand on her hip. "You like it?"

The point they were at was perfect for viewing the higher mountains in the distance. "It's beautiful."

"Seems like a whole different world, doesn't it?" Boone stared out across the space, his expression relaxing.

"How did you find this?"

He shrugged. "I got tired of the same trails so I started to venture out." Boone tipped his head to the view in front of them. "I found this one day and kept coming back."

"I can see why."

"Here." Boone worked the pack off her back. He unzipped it and pulled out a rolled-up canvas-lined mat. After shaking it open he flipped it across the small bit of flat space around them. "Now you can sit and relax."

"Is that what you do when you come up here?" It wasn't as hard to imagine Boone up here as it would have been a few weeks ago. Before she would have never expected him to own a pair of hiking boots, let alone put them to use. "Just sit here?" She settled down on the soft flannel side of the thick blanket.

He eased down beside her, situating his body close enough to hers that their sides touched. "I sit here and think."

Mae studied his profile. "Should I ask what you think about?"

"I'm pretty sure you already know." Boone turned her way. "Unless you need to hear it."

Maybe she did.

His body shifted, angling her way. "When I left here I didn't really know who I was, Mae." He reached out to catch some of the hair that always worked free from her braid. "But I knew I wasn't ready to be what you needed me to be."

"What was it you thought I needed?"

"I promised you we were getting married and having kids. I promised I was going to take care of you." His hand dropped to the ground. "I was going to have to be a husband. A dad." His eyes fell. "I was just a kid. I didn't know the first damn thing about how to be a man. "Boone sucked in a breath. "I knew I was going to disappoint you, Mae. I figured it was better if I just did it and got it over with."

"I was a kid too, Boone." She inched her hand along the blanket between them until the tips of her fingers touched his. "I didn't expect you to know it all or be ready to do it all." She swallowed down an old pain that had never really gone away, no matter what she accomplished. No matter what she tried to cover it with. "I just wanted you to be there with me while we figured it out."

When his eyes lifted to hers the pain there was as clear as the mountains in the distance. "I don't know how to fix what I did."

Before she would have said there was no way he could.

No way to repair the damage he'd done walking away like he did.

But that was before she knew exactly why he left.

It was still stupid. It was still immature and selfish.

But it was very different from what she'd believed all these years.

"Honestly, I don't know either." Mae traced the line of his knuckles with one finger. "But it can't hurt to try."

Boone's free hand came to her face, sliding over her cheek with a solid touch that was still so soft.

So careful.

He leaned close, cradling her face as his head tipped against hers. "I can promise you that I will do more than try, Sweetheart." His lips brushed hers in a kiss that was as gentle as his touch.

She scooted closer, wrapping one arm around the width of his broad shoulders.

The hand at her cheek moved back, tangling in her collapsing braid as Boone eased her back onto the blanket. His lips moved to her neck, nipping at her skin. She arched against him, already craving more of whatever he would give her.

His large frame pressed into her, covering her. Surrounding her.

Made her feel protected. Hidden in spite of the fact that they were outside in front of God and everybody.

The new leaves made soft rattling noises as a soft breeze

moved in from the mountains, stirring the smells of the woods. Mixing them with the scent of the man holding her close.

"You still smell the same." Mae ran her nose along his shoulder, breathing deep as she reached the warm skin of his neck.

"I still wear the same cologne you bought me." Boone leaned up, bracing himself on one arm. "I tried some other ones but I never liked them as much as this one."

Mae traced her fingers along his chest, following the dips and lines of the muscles that he'd developed quite a bit more than she'd realized. "That's because I have good taste."

"I'm not sure about that." Boone leaned down to kiss her again, this time tracing her tongue with his before lifting away. "You're here with me."

She started to laugh but an odd sound stopped her.

Mae stared up at Boone's face as the odd sound continued.

His whole body went still as his eyes held hers. "Don't move."

Mae rolled her eyes to the side where the odd sound was coming from.

Her stomach dropped and her heart started to race.

"Shhh." Boone's tone was low and soft. "Just stay quiet."

The rattling sound she'd thought was the leaves continued as the snake stared them down.

"He'll go away. You just got to give him a minute to get over himself." Boone's thumb stroked her cheek but other than that he didn't move.

It was difficult to see well without turning her head, but

there was no way she was risking it. If she moved there was a chance Boone would end up with a snake bite.

Because there was no way he would let the snake bite her.

Mae's eyes came back to Boone's face. His eyes were still on her, holding steady. She let the air out of her lungs in a careful exhale as the rate of her pulse slowed.

The rattling grew quieter.

Boone's head slowly tipped in the direction of the snake. His eyes scanned the rocky area the reptile escaped to. "I'm going to take that as a sign we should head back."

"But now it's in the woods." Mae grabbed onto Boone as he started to lift up. "We could step right on him."

"He went down the slope. Rattlers like open area and rocks. He's just lookin' for a good spot to get a little heat before the sun goes down." Boone pulled her up as he stood. "We'll be just fine. I promise."

Mae rested one hand on her stomach as it started to roll.

"Mae." Boone bunched the blanket up and tucked it under one arm as he reached out to tip her chin with his pointer in a move that dragged her eyes from where they were scanning the tree line. "Everything is okay. Trust me."

The last two words stopped her short.

Could she trust him?

If not, none of this mattered.

Mae took another look in the direction the snake had been. "Okay."

Boone smiled. "Okay." He shoved the blanket into the backpack before tucking it back onto her shoulders. "But just in case I'm going to haul you out of here." He crouched down, once again lifting her onto his back.

"What? You just said he was gone." Mae tucked her feet up higher as Boone stepped into the thick brush. She tipped her head to one side, then the other, squinting through the branches and leaves.

"I know what I said." Boone was moving pretty quickly. "Keep your ears open."

Mae pressed her lips together and held on tighter as she strained to listen to every sound around them.

Boone didn't put her down until they were well down the trail, where it opened up to a decent width and visibility was better. She smacked at him. "You told me to trust you."

"I asked you to trust me." He grabbed her hand as she tried to smack at him again. "And I appreciate that you did."

"You said he was gone." She shot him a glare.

"That's not what I said." Boone pulled her close as the lot and his truck came into view. "I said everything was okay."

She frowned up at him, struggling to hold the expression in the face of Boone's wide grin. "And I believed you."

"Because it's the truth." Boone kept his arms around her as he walked them toward the truck. "Everything is okay."

"Hmph." Her smile snuck its way to the edges of her mouth, lifting them in spite of her best efforts.

He chuckled as he leaned in, nuzzling her neck. "Does this mean we don't need to go shopping for a pair of hiking boots?"

"I might have to think on that a little more."

Boone held her close with one arm as he opened the truck door with the other. He took the backpack as she climbed in, sliding the bag into the backseat as she buckled up.

Boone pulled out of the lot and turned in the opposite direction of town.

Mae looked down the road then to Boone. "Where are we going?"

"The ranch." He reached for her hand again, immediately pulling it to his lips. "I figured you'd want to see how Camille's doing."

CHAPTER FIFTEEN

"HAVE YOU SEEN her?"

"I checked on her last night and again this morning." Boone knew Mae would want to know how Camille was doing and he'd wanted to be sure he could tell her. "She and Cal are both as okay as they can be right now."

"Are they staying in one of the cabins?"

"Hell no." Boone smiled. "They're already set up at The Inn."

"There are rooms finished at The Inn?"

He thought for sure his mother would have dragged Mae back to show off the place. Especially now that they were finally in the finishing stages after months of delays. "Have you not been there?"

Mae shook her head, lips pressed together. "I didn't really like being at the ranch any more than I had to."

"Worried you'd run into me?"

"With my car."

He laughed. "I might have let you do it."

Mae's expression softened. "It was easier to be mad at you."

"You can always be mad at me when I'm a dumbass." It made him happy that she didn't forgive him too easily. Meant Mae knew she didn't have to.

Mae was quiet for a minute. "I wouldn't have done that before." Her voice was low as she looked out the window. "I would have gone along with anything you said or did."

"I know." Boone focused on the feel of her hand in his. "And I wasn't strong enough to handle that pressure."

"Now you think you are?"

"Nope." He shook his head a little. "Don't have to. Now I think you will question everything." His eyes stayed on her. "Including how I breathe at night."

Mae's lips moved to one side in a wry smile. "Is that your way of telling me you snore?"

He shrugged. "Hell if I know."

"If you did someone would have told you." Mae reached up to catch a piece of hair snagged on her lips.

"No one around to tell me." He turned back to the road. "Not one for sleepovers."

Mae went still. Her eyes peeked his way. "Oh." Her hand fell to her lap as she stared straight ahead.

The truth was something he had to feed her in small bits. Too much at once would overwhelm her.

Make her feel like he was cornering her.

Because at this point he was all in.

Had been forever, just wasn't willing to admit it until the life he'd been chasing seemed possible.

Mae didn't say anything else the rest of the ride to the

ranch, just sat in the spot that was always meant to be hers, the sweet smell of her skin filling the air.

They pulled up just as dinner would be finishing up. That meant the whole family would be inside the farmhouse to see what he'd done.

Who he'd brought.

"Is she here?" Mae eyed the farmhouse, her uncertainty clear.

"If you think my mother hasn't figured out how to suck Camille and Calvin into the family then you've definitely forgotten what she's like." Boone jumped out of the truck and rounded to Mae's side to pull her door open. "Come on."

"Maybe we can just go back to The Inn and wait for them to come back there."

"If I can handle this then you sure as hell can handle it." Boone reached one hand out to her. "Come on. I'll protect you from her."

"It's not that I need to be protected." Mae's gaze went back to the porch. "She's just—"

"A lot. I know." He wiggled his fingers. "Come on. It'll take some of the heat off Camille."

Mae's head spun his way as she shot him a glare. "That was dirty."

"And worked like a charm." He grinned as Mae grabbed his hand and jumped out of the truck. The second her feet hit the gravel she tried to pull her hand away but he held tight.

"You're mother's going to think—"

"My mother's going to think I have a death wish." Boone leaned close to press a kiss to Mae's temple.

"She's going to think we're—"

The front door flew open and Maryann Pace stepped out

onto the porch, eyes narrowed as she wiped her hands on the apron tied around her waist. "Dinner's over."

"Didn't come for dinner. Brought Mae to see Camille."

On cue, Camille stepped out onto the porch with Clara close behind. The second Camille's eyes landed on Mae her shoulders dropped on a sigh of relief Boone completely understood.

It was just as overwhelming to be on his mother's good side as it was to be on her bad side.

His mother lifted a brow. "Interesting."

Mae's feet moved slower and slower the closer they got to the porch. Boone gave her hand a squeeze, hoping to ease whatever upset was slowing her down.

Clara stepped forward, one of the twins perched on her hip. "You want some blueberry cobbler?" She grinned at Mae. "We've got ice cream too."

Mae's steps seemed to come a little easier. "Darn it, Clara." She almost smiled. "I might have a little."

Clara leaned into Michaela's ear, smiling wide at Mae. "Miss Mae loves ice cream. That's how you can get her to do whatever you want."

"Speaking of." Mae climbed the steps, dropping his hand as she went straight for her friends. "I made that lemon pie you wanted to try."

"You are my favorite person right now." Clara turned to go inside with Mae moving in behind her. "At least until I try to fit in the wedding dress I bought."

"So does that mean you don't want me to bring you some pie?"

"It means I will just not breathe at the wedding." Clara set Michaela on her feet and the little girl immediately took off, racing to the front room where Wyatt and Calvin were sitting with Bill watching cartoons. She smiled softly as they walked past, making their way to the kitchen.

Boone was about to follow along when his mother snatched his arm, yanking him back. "What in the hell are you doing?"

"I brought Mae to see Camille. She was worried about her."

The frown on his mother's face deepened. "You know that's not what I mean."

"Boone?" Mae stood in the doorway, a container of ice cream in one hand and a scooper in the other. "You want to dish out the ice cream?"

If there was any sign that would tell him Mae was working in the same direction he was, it was this moment.

"I'd love to dish out the ice cream." He left his mother standing in the hall, staring at his back with a look he knew well.

And right now he couldn't care less.

Because Mae just came to his rescue.

He took the freezing pail from her, leaning in close. "I owe you one."

"I'm counting that as at least five." She smiled up at him.

"Make it ten."

"Now you're just being cocky." Mae shoved the scooper his way. "Go dish up dessert."

Brody was at the counter spooning cobbler into bowls. His brows lifted when he saw Boone. "Surprised to see you here."

Boone stood beside his older brother, setting the

container of vanilla on the counter and peeling back the lid. "I live here."

"Hasn't seemed like it the last few nights."

"I've been busy."

"I heard about that." Boone tipped his head toward the bruise blooming across his cheek. "Rumor has it Junior got one up on you."

"He took advantage of an opportunity."

"Isn't that the exact definition of *got one up*?"

"Boone was keeping me from killing Junior with a metal table." Mae took the first loaded bowl of cobbler and walked away, passing it to Calvin where he was seated at the table next to Wyatt.

Brody turned to Boone, brows high on his forehead. "That part was left out."

"Junior shoved Mae off the porch." Boone kept his voice low enough there was no chance anyone else could hear. "She wasn't happy and definitely planned to knock a little more than the sense out of him."

Brody grinned. "I knew I liked her."

"She's something else." It was getting harder and harder to think about the Mae he used to know and the Mae he knew now as the same person. There were similarities, sure.

But so much was different.

"You're gonna have to pick up the pace, boys." Maryann snagged the next three bowls. "Instead of flapping your jaws." She glared at both of them.

"Thanks." Brody slammed the next bowl into Boone's chest. "Now she's gonna be hell on wheels for the rest of the night."

"It was going to happen sooner or later." Boone added ice cream to the dish and lined it down the counter.

Brooks came in through the back door, stopping short when he saw Boone at the counter. His eyes slowly went to where Mae was at the table helping Clara and Camille with the kids. They came back Boone's way.

Then he turned and walked right back out.

"Pussy." Boone dropped in another scoop of ice cream.

"He's trying to stay on Mom's good side."

"Why's that?"

"You seen the new interior decorator?" Brody glanced up at their mother.

"Probably. I don't remember."

"You'd remember." Brody eyed him. "Hell. Maybe at this point you wouldn't." He loaded up the final two bowls of cobbler. "You're probably too far gone already."

"Probably." Boone added an extra scoop of ice cream to one of the two bowls and carried it to where Mae was listening to a very animated story about how Leah sent a chicken down the slide of their new playset.

"And she flapped her wings like this." Leah flung her arms around, nearly knocking Wyatt's spoon out of his mouth.

"Does the chicken like going down the slide?"

Leah's eyes rolled toward Clara and back to Mae. "Cla-La says no."

"Cla-La is right." Maryann passed a napkin to Leah. "And we want our chickens to be happy so they keep laying us eggs, right?"

Leah was quiet for a minute as she looked back toward Clara. Finally she sighed. "Right."

Mae pressed out the smile on her lips.

"Here." Boone handed over the bowl with extra ice cream.

Mae looked down at the double scoops. "If I didn't know better I'd think you were trying to get me to do something."

He lifted one shoulder in a half-shrug as he took a bite of the cobbler. Boone backed to where his dad and brothers were congregated at one end of the dining room, giving Mae a little space.

Brett was oddly quiet as they ate. Bill and Brody talked with Boone about their plans for tomorrow and what needed to be done, but Brett didn't say a single word.

Which was very unusual.

Their dad peered around the full dining room. "Where's Brooks?"

"He ran away when he saw Boone and Mae here." Brody grinned as he leaned back against the edge of the peninsula between the dining room and kitchen.

Bill turned to Boone. "Pretty big risk you're taking there, son."

"I know."

"Not sure you do."

Boone straightened. Their father wasn't one to meddle, so his interest in the topic was unexpected. "Tell me then."

"Women are pack creatures, son." He tipped his head toward the group at the other end of the room. "You just made it clear to all of them that you had certain intentions with one of their pack." Bill gave his head a little shake. "You mess up and your mother will be the least of your worries."

"I'm not going to mess up." He'd spent years waiting for

this chance. Working to be what he wished he'd been a decade ago.

"I sure as hell hope not." His father tipped back the rest of the milk in his glass. "'Cause I'm not so interested in dealing with the lot of them when they come looking for you."

"Hey." Clara hollered across the room, her eyes on Boone. "We're going back to The Inn so Mae can see it." Her gaze was steady and shockingly intimidating considering how sweet the woman was. "You all get to clean up the kitchen."

"Yes, ma'am." Boone tipped his head in a nod.

The women all filtered out, leaving the mess and the kids behind.

"You boys ready to learn the most important part of being a cowboy?" Bill took his glass and bowl and headed toward the kitchen.

Wyatt was already on his feet, eyes bright with the chance to learn more from one of his favorite people. "Yeah."

Bill shot him a grin. "It's doin' as you're told."

Wyatt carried his bowl and spoon straight to the dishwasher, but Bill stopped him. "We're not leavin' more work for the ladies later." He switched on the water and squirted in some soap. "We're gonna wash, dry, and put away." He winked at Calvin. "It makes your Nanna happy, and a happy wife means a happy life."

Calvin's gaze stayed on Bill as he stood at the sink scrubbing dishes and passing them to Brody to dry. Boone was last in line, putting them away while Brett wiped down counters and packed up the leftovers.

The little boys brought in the dirty dishes and helped juggle Leah and Michaela.

Once the work was done Bill went to Calvin's side, giving him a pat on the back. "I think you're going to make a heck of a cowboy."

Calvin's eyes dipped to the floor. "Thanks."

The line of Bill's jaw tightened for just a second before softening. "You kiddos ready to go watch our shows?"

Every evening the kids sat with their dad in the living room, watching a couple cartoons and playing together.

Calvin was the last to leave the kitchen. He turned to look back at Brett.

Brett gave him a thumbs-up.

Calvin almost seemed to nod before turning to follow the rest of the crew into the front of the house.

"How's he doing?" Brody folded the towel he'd used for drying and hung it over the handle of the dishwasher to dry.

Brett's expression was tight. "About like you'd expect." He crossed his arms, leaning back against the counter. "As good as this place can be for him it's still a lot. He's overwhelmed. Not sure where he fits in."

"At least he's talkin' about it." Brody scratched at one cheek. "Better than him being shut down."

"Might still happen." Brett was the most easy-going of his brothers. It was strange to see him so serious.

"He's got a good momma." Boone saw how Camille put herself between Junior and Calvin firsthand. "She'll do anything to protect him."

Brett's nostrils flared. "She shouldn't have to."

"Hopefully that's over now." Brody smirked. "Pretty confident even Junior's dumbass knows what her bein' here means."

Brett tipped his head toward Boone. "Except that one

made it seem like maybe we weren't as capable of dishing out an ass-kicking as we used to be."

Boone held his hands out at his sides. "He took a cheap shot when I was taking a metal table away from Mae. Did you want me to let her hit him with it? She'd probably would have killed him. Then what?"

"Then he'd be dead and we wouldn't have to worry about any of this."

"And Mae would be in a heap of trouble." Boone shook his head. "That's not happening when I can stop it."

Brett eyed him. "That mean what I think it means?"

"Depends on what you think it means."

Brody looked Boone up and down. "You think you're ready for her?"

Boone tipped his head in a single nod. "Yup."

Brody crossed his arms over his chest, a smile working onto his mouth. "Should be interesting then.

"How's that?"

He lifted his shoulders. "Now we get to see if Mae's ready for you."

CHAPTER SIXTEEN

"THIS IS BEAUTIFUL." Mae walked through the kitchen at The Inn, sliding one finger across the smooth marble countertops. "I'm so excited for you."

"My life is hardly anything to be excited about right now." Camille smiled at Mae. "Yours though..."

Mae glanced to where Clara and Maryann were in the front room discussing the interior designer's suggestions for the window coverings. "I'm not sure there's anything to be excited about in mine either."

Camille's brows went up. "I saw you holding Boone's hand. That's pretty exciting."

That was the least exciting thing she'd done with Boone in the past couple of days. "I don't know what I'm doing."

"I'm hoping that's how life works. Otherwise I'm screwed." Camille straightened the large wicker basket sitting on the counter. "Because I have no clue what I'm doing."

"You're getting a fresh start." Camille's situation was pretty cut and dry. "You're finally moving forward."

"So we're in the same place then." Camille's comment held an edge of challenge.

Mae opened her mouth to argue. She'd been sure there was no way she could just start over with Boone.

That she'd never be able to forget what he'd done.

And she probably couldn't. But now felt nothing like then.

Not anymore.

"I'm so glad I finally got you to come out here." Maryann swept into the room, a pride-filled smile lighting up her face. "What do you think?"

"It's amazing." Mae lifted her eyes to the soaring ceilings. "You're going to be packed."

"I hope so, otherwise Bill is going to die." Maryann propped her hands on her hips as she stared out the back windows, her smile falling to a frown.

Mae turned to look in the same direction.

A familiar horse carried a familiar man across the field at the other side of the in-ground pool spanning the back of the building.

Camille leaned into her side, voice low as she whispered in her ear. "You're smiling."

Mae pressed her lips together, trying to flatten them. "He's probably ready to take me home."

"I'm sure that's it." Camille's tone dripped with sarcasm.

Mae turned to Maryann. "This place is gorgeous. I'm so excited for you."

Maryann caught her hands, holding them tight. "Thank you, honey." Her eyes became laser focused. "You're a smart girl with the whole world at your feet. You can have anything you want, understand?"

Mae offered a smile. "I do."

Maryann's smile came back. "Good." She used her grip to pull Mae in for a tight hug. "I am so proud of all you've accomplished."

"Thank you." Mae swallowed around an unwanted lump. The second Maryann let her go she backed toward the door. "I'll see you guys later."

"I'm sure you will." Camille grinned her way.

Mae spun away and hurried out the door, rushing away from the reminder of exactly what all would come along with Boone.

Because the man definitely had baggage, and now it included two of her friends.

She skirted the edge of the pool as Boone and Nellie trotted along the fence surrounding it. She pointed to a cluster of evergreen bushes. "That where you puked?"

"I saved a child's life and all my mother could tell you was how I puked in her bushes?"

Mae smiled. "I'm not sure she's convinced you're a good catch."

Boone reached one hand down to her. "There's only one woman I'm trying to convince, remember?"

Mae looked from his outstretched hand to his face. "Where are we going?"

"Back to my truck. I figured you'd be ready to go home."

"Why didn't you drive back here?"

"I had to go check on something I can't reach by truck." Boone wiggled his fingers. "You comin' or you want me to go get the truck and come back for you?" His eyes lifted to where the three women inside were all staring their way. "I'm sure they'd be happy to chat with you some more."

Mae immediately grabbed his hand, letting him pull her up and onto the saddle in front of him as he scooted off the back. "Is this going to hurt her?"

"Not this one time." Boone gripped the back of the saddle, passing the reins off to Mae. "But if you're going to make a habit of coming out here then we'll have to get you a horse of your own."

"A habit?" She turned to face him as Nellie started toward the cabins. "You're the one who brought me here."

"You sayin' you weren't planning to come out on your own?"

She was. "Not to see you."

"Doesn't matter why. Just that you were." Boone leaned closer, resting one hand on her thigh as they closed the short distance to the cabins. "How's Camille?"

"She didn't really seem interested in talking about it." Mae shrugged. "I guess I can't blame her."

"I heard Junior's out already." Boone's body moved along with Nellie's. "His momma and daddy posted his bail."

"Of course they did." Mae sighed. "I wonder if they bothered to check on Camille or Calvin."

"Not everyone is like your parents and mine, Mae." Boone's deep voice was soft.

Mae leaned back a little as Nellie's even gait and the quiet of the pastures around them relaxed her. "If Camille's parents were alive I bet things would have been different."

"Maybe." Boone's chest met her back. "But things can still be different for her. It's never too late."

"I hope so." She tipped her head to peek back at him. "Thank you for checking on her."

"That's not something you have to thank me for." Boone

reached out to cover her hand with his, using the strap of leather to direct Nellie toward the barn.

"Not everyone would do it, though." Mae stared up at his face.

The face of the man who took the place of the boy she once knew.

Once loved.

"Something wrong?"

She shook her head. "You just look different."

"You're still not used to seeing me without the hat." He smiled down at her.

"It doesn't really have anything to do with the hat." It wasn't quite like seeing him for the first time.

But it was close.

Boone pulled Nellie to a stop right outside the barn. "I think you're just tired." He eased out from behind her, dropping down to the ground before reaching one hand her way. "Come on. Let's get you home."

Mae carefully swung one leg over and down, making sure she didn't hit Boone in the process. She turned to face him. "Can I use your bathroom?"

Boone tipped his head toward one of the cabins. "I'll put Nellie down for the night." He moved away almost immediately, disappearing into the barn.

Mae turned toward the cabin Boone called home.

It was tiny. Not much more than a decent-sized shed.

She went up the stairs to the small covered porch. A chair sat on each side of the centered door, looking toward the main house she could barely see in the distance.

This is what he came home to?

Boone spent almost a decade as the PRCA all-around

champion. Unless he blew through money as fast as he made it there was no reason for him to live in a place like this.

Unless he believed he deserved to live in a place like this.

Mae turned back toward the barn.

What would it be like to spend a decade kicking yourself for making a bad decision?

What would it be like to wake up every morning wishing you'd made a different one?

Wishing you'd been better?

Mae twisted the knob on the door and stepped into Boone's home. A small lamp in one corner lit the single room of the space. Two twin beds sat on opposite walls.

He could have at least shoved them together.

A small table and a few chairs sat at one side of the front door and a mini fridge and microwave sat opposite it on a wooden hutch.

There was no sign of his time away from Moss Creek. None of the awards she knew he won. No pictures of him in action.

Nothing.

Mae walked between the beds to the back of the cabin. A closet at the end of one of the beds was filled with neatly-hung clothes. Across from it was a door leading to a small bathroom. She flipped on the light and went in, closing the door behind her.

Over the years she'd imagined the glamorous life Boone left her for. The excitement. The fame.

As painful as it was to think she wasn't enough for him, the truth hurt almost as much. She'd put everything she had into being with him, never once considering what it would be like for him to try to live up to her expectations.

And why would she? She was a kid.

Just like him.

Mae finished her reasons for being there, washing her hands with soap that smelled like Boone and drying them on his towel before going out.

He stood just inside the front door. "You ready to go?"

Mae's eyes drifted around the space. Around this place that wasn't a home of any sort.

It was a punishment. Punishment for something that maybe didn't warrant it.

She shook her head. "I don't want to go."

Boone went perfectly still as she walked toward him, each step making her more certain of what she did want.

Mae stopped right in front of him. "I want to stay here." She reached out to run the tips of her fingers across the soft fabric of his t-shirt. "With you."

"I'm not sure that's an option just yet, Sweetheart."

"Why not?" She climbed her fingertips up the center of his chest. "I'm plenty old enough to decide what I want."

"I don't want to rush this, Mae." He caught her hand, lifting it until his lips brushed the inside of her wrist. "I want you to be sure."

"I'm sure I want to stay with you." Her breath caught as his lips made another pass across her skin.

"That's not what I need you to be sure about." Boone pulled her hand closer, running his mouth along her inner arm as he lifted her palm to his shoulder. "I'm not here for anything less than everything, Mae."

"What's everything?" She could barely whisper the question out.

"Everything's everything." Boone trailed the fingers of

one hand up the arm still hanging at her side. His broad body moved in closer. "I want it all." His hand moved over her shoulder and up her neck, the warm drag of his skin over hers lifting goosebumps across her skin. "I want to make good on every promise I ever made you."

"I don't need you to take care of me." She collected his shirt, gathering it up with her fingers. "I know how to take care of myself now."

His expression was difficult to read in the dim light, but his shoulders slumped the tiniest bit.

"We can't be what we once were." Mae moved the hand on Boone's shoulder, feeling along the thick band of muscles as she went. "But we can't really start over either."

"So where does that leave us?"

Her eyes lifted to meet his. "Right here. Trying to figure it out together."

He chuckled softly, the sound more akin to an exhale than an actual laugh. "I came back here thinking you'd be just as perfect as you were when I left." Boone's eyes were dark on hers. "I never expected you would be better."

She'd worked hard to be the best version of herself. To show all she was capable of.

Never once did she expect Boone's acknowledgment of that would sit so warm and solid in her belly.

Mae edged in closer to him, the hand in his shirt dipping under the hem to graze the flat plane of his stomach. "You might be a little better too."

"Hopefully I'm a lot better, otherwise you should cut your losses and run."

Loss was a word she was familiar with. One she always attributed to Boone.

But now that seemed wrong.

Maybe not wrong so much as lagging. It was a loss at the beginning. One she turned into an opportunity to gain.

To grow.

And it seemed like she wasn't the only one.

"I don't want to run." Mae closed the last bit of space between them, pushing up on her toes. "I want to stay right here."

"It's late."

"Does that mean you want to take me home?"

"It means if you stay much longer you might not get home until morning."

"I thought you didn't do sleepovers."

Boone's lips curved into a slow smile. "You are always the exception, Mae."

His arms banded across her back, pulling her body tight to his as his mouth caught hers. Boone slowly walked her backward toward the bed closest to the closet. He took her down to the mattress with a slow slant of his body. Her back hit the surprisingly uncomfortable surface, but she didn't have time to dwell on it before Boone's body pressed her deeper into the lumpy firmness.

The bed frame creaked at their combined weight, groaning a little each time one of them moved.

But it was the least interesting thing happening in the world right now.

Mae held Boone's face in her hands as he kissed her, his lips passing over hers until her breath wasn't enough. She tried to pull in more air as his mouth moved away, over her neck while his hands worked her shirt up. She grabbed at Boone, the need to feel his skin on hers building more with each second there was still something left between them.

Her own needs weren't anything she worried too much about in her day-to-day life. There wasn't time.

And boy was that coming back to bite her right now.

Because right now the needs she'd been ignoring were making their presence known. Even after last night.

Hell. Maybe last night made it worse. Reminded her of all she'd been missing lately.

All she might have if she was willing to take a leap of faith.

And it was time to jump.

Mae tugged his shirt with both hands. "Take this off."

Boone's chin caught in the neckline as she wrestled the soft jersey over his head. His weight suddenly left hers. Boone pushed up on his knees where they straddled her hips. He grabbed the shirt she'd been fighting, pulling it off in one easy motion.

"Holy shit." It came out all on its own.

Boone cocked a brow at her as one wide hand moved across the rippled skin of his stomach.

He had freaking abs. Perfect lines of definition she could clearly count like sheep if she had a hard time falling asleep at night.

The sight of them sent heat creeping over her skin and between her thighs. It put visions of those same abs flexing as he thrust his hips so deep in her mind they might never come out again.

They made her needy.

They made her a little crazy.

And they made her a lot greedy.

She reached for him, grabbing Boone by the waistband of the athletic pants she hadn't been so sure about.

Her opinion on them was changing quickly.

Because they were much easier to work with than jeans.

She barely had one hand in the front of them, the tips of her fingers brushing across the straining length she intended to free, when Boone gripped her wrist and lifted it high over her head, pinning it to the mattress.

He shook his head at her as his body came down over hers, eyes dark. "That's not how this is going to go, Sweetheart."

CHAPTER SEVENTEEN

MAE STARED UP at him. "Who said you got to decide how this goes?"

"You want it to be fun, right?"

Mae's eyes dipped, skimming down his chest. "I would like to participate in the fun."

"But the more fun you have the shorter the ride's gonna be."

"Are you saying you don't work well under pressure?" One brow lifted in a challenging arc.

"I'm saying you should realize a man has limits, and you are one hell of a limit."

"If you think I'm going to lay back and think of England then you're going to be very disappointed."

"Disappointed is probably the wrong word." Boone snagged her other hand as it went for his straining dick. "Embarrassed is probably more accurate."

Mae wiggled under him, twisting her body to rub against the part she clearly wanted to use against him. "Maybe women like to be so sexy a man can't hold back."

"You should be proud then." Boone leaned down to run his nose along her neck. "Because if you had your way I'd be coming in your hand right about now."

Her sharp inhale at the admission made him a little bolder. "You like a little dirty talk, Mae?"

"You probably shouldn't dish it out if you can't take it." Her eyes rolled his way. "I don't remember you handling it well last time I wanted you to fuck me."

Damn.

Her lips curved in a smile that made it clear she could bring him down even with her hands tied behind her back.

"What's wrong, Cowboy?" Mae twisted under him again, dragging her body against him, breasts and belly teasing him with the softness she possessed. "You look worried."

He shook his head. "Not worried." Boone scanned her from head to toe. "Just strategizing."

"Better make it good because you've got to let me go sooner or later." She wiggled her fingers. "And I will definitely be ready when you do."

"You're the one who'll suffer, Sweetheart." He clamped one hand around both her wrists, pinning them in place. "Because if you want fucked then I've got to make it that far."

Mae's eyes darkened and her lids got heavy. "I definitely want that."

"What if we make a deal?" He didn't expect their first time together would result in almost immediate bargaining, but he was running out of options fast, especially with Mae's expanded vocabulary. "This time you behave. Next time you can do whatever you want."

She looked suspicious. "You'll just lay there and take it?"

"I'll just lay there and take it." The thought of Mae taking what she wanted from him was about the most appealing thing he could imagine. It tightened his balls almost instantly and had his dick throbbing with the need for friction. Some sort of contact to ease the ache there.

Mae's eyes held his. "Deal." She stopped trying to wiggle out of his grip and her body relaxed a little. "What's your plan now?"

He had no plan outside of doing whatever it took to get her off as many times as possible. Make sure she knew he wasn't as amateurish as she claimed to remember.

"Now I'm gonna make you come." Boone shoved up her shirt, taking it all the way over her head before unhooking the front clasp of her bra. As soon as the cups fell away he caught one nipple in his mouth, sucking it deep before letting it fall free. "Then I'm gonna make it happen again." He moved to the other breast as he worked the fly of her pants open. "And if I can manage it I'm going to get one more out of you." He shoved one hand into the waistband, sliding under the hot pink lace of her panties. "Then I'll do what you want me to."

Her hips lifted, closing the gap between his fingers and her pussy. She gasped softly as his skin brushed hers. "You're shooting for the rafters right out of the gate, aren't you?"

"I've got big goals, Sweetheart." He pressed deeper, sliding between the wet heat of her labia to find the swollen nub of her clit. "A man doesn't get where he wants to go without setting the bar high."

Mae hummed as he worked her clit with the pads of his fingers. "Then I've got sad news for you." She grabbed his wrist, stopping his movement. "Because I'm a one and done sort of girl."

"I am planning to correct that." He fought against her hold.

Mae was suddenly very serious. "There's nothing to be corrected. I'm not broken."

Boone stilled. "You're not the one I'm saying was the issue."

"I know what you're saying." Mae's chin lifted. "But how would you feel if I told you we couldn't have sex unless you got me off three times?" Her head barely shook. "It's not fair to put that pressure on me."

Damn.

He didn't even have her naked and he'd already fucked up. Boone pulled his hand free of her pants as he eased his body over hers. "I'm sorry. I just want this to be—"

"Just let it be what it's going to be."

"I want it to be perfect for you."

Mae reached up to stroke along his cheek with the tips of her fingers. "I don't expect perfect from you."

"You deserve it."

"What about you? What do you deserve?" Her touch trailed down his jaw, the fingers of both hands sliding down his neck. "I'm not interested in doing this if you want to make it all about me."

"It should be all about you."

Mae's palms flattened against his breastbone, warm and soft as they pressed against his skin. "You can't punish yourself forever."

"I can."

"What are you really punishing yourself for?" Mae's eyes searched his. "For being a kid who was scared? For leaving instead of doing something you weren't ready for?"

"I should have stayed and been a man about it."

"What does that even mean? You think marrying your high school sweetheart and playing house makes you a man? Because that's what Junior did and I wouldn't ever classify him as a man."

"I should have stayed and done everything I promised to do."

Mae's eyes dipped down to where her hands rested over his heart. "I don't remember anyone mentioning there was a time limit on what you offered me."

He'd hoped for forgiveness.

Understanding was not even a consideration.

He should have known better.

"I never stopped loving you, Mae."

"That would make sense." She stroked down his stomach. "I make really good pie."

A pressure he didn't realize was in his chest eased. "You're coming real close to gettin' more pie jokes."

Mae's head tipped back on a laugh, light and easy and everything he needed in that moment.

This was what he came back for.

Being with Mae was always so easy.

So right.

She pretended he was funny.

Made him feel understood.

Appreciated.

Loved.

And for the first time it seemed like maybe it could be that way again.

He stroked across her cheek. "I missed you so damn much."

It was something he knew he had no right to say since he was the one at fault. The reason he had to miss her in the first place.

Mae's expression was soft. "Good." She leaned up, pressing her lips to his as one arm hooked around his neck, taking him to the mattress with her.

She was so soft under him. All warm curves and smooth skin. He wanted to explore every inch of her. Claim it all as his own.

Because she was the single thing that brought him back to Moss Creek.

The single thing that kept him moving forward when nothing made him happy. When there was no one who understood.

When even he didn't understand.

It was always her that drove him forward. Made him strive to be better.

To find his way back to this place.

He held her close, running his hands over her arms, her stomach, her hips. Fighting the rest of her clothes off, each move getting less controlled.

And more desperate.

He wanted every bit of her against every bit of him, and he couldn't make it happen fast enough.

Mae kicked at her pants as she shoved at the waistband of his, pushing them down past his hips. The second her legs were free they came around him. "Boone, please."

He fumbled around like the kid he was ten years ago, struggling to get to the condoms he'd stashed under his bed two nights ago when he was feeling optimistic. "Hang on."

The damn package wasn't even open so he needed both hands. Unfortunately, Mae wasn't making the job any easier.

One hand closed around his straining dick, stroking it in long sweeps of her fist.

He sucked in a breath through clenched teeth as the box dropped to the floor.

"Boone." Her tone was urgent.

He leaned, trying to snag the box from where it had rolled almost to the edge of the other bed. His fingers brushed the corner.

He stretched a little more.

And went over the side.

His back hit the wood floor. Mae yelped and a heartbeat later her body hit his. She blinked down at him.

Then she started to laugh. Her eyes went to the box he'd been fighting with. She pushed up to her knees and snagged it off the floor, turning the unopened pack in her hands. "You probably should have opened these already."

"I didn't want to get ahead of myself."

"Bet you're regretting that decision now."

"It can go on the list of decisions I regret."

Mae snapped the top open and pulled out a strip, tearing one off. "Maybe it's time you stopped worrying about it." She ripped across the foil and pulled out the condom. "Maybe everything worked out exactly how it was supposed to." She rolled the condom down his length before leaning toward him, resting both palms flat on the floor at either side of his head. "Maybe this is exactly where we're supposed to be."

"This is definitely not where you are supposed to be, Sweetheart." Boone wrapped one arm around her waist, hefting Mae against his chest as he pushed up from the floor.

He'd give up a lot of what he'd imagined this time would be like.

But there was no fucking way it was happening on a dirty cabin floor.

Boone rolled them onto the tiny bed, his arms and legs tangling with hers as he tried to find some leverage to work with on the narrow mattress. The thing was definitely not made for these kinds of activities. It would be lucky to survive until morning.

Mae smiled as she laced her fingers into his hair, pulling his face down to hers, sighing into his mouth as he slid along her pussy. Her hips lifted into him, making it damn near impossible to avoid the inevitable any longer.

"Please, Boone." Her whispered plea was the last straw, breaking him in ways he didn't know were possible.

Breaking his rules.

Shattering his plans.

Crumbling the foundation he intended to build.

Leaving him stripped bare. Nothing to offer her but what he was in this moment.

He pressed against her, holding back with all he had, trying to find some focus.

But there was none to be had.

She was his only focus. Her smell. Her taste. The way she sighed his name as he eased forward, inching into her with the remaining control he managed to possess.

Mae arched under him, her body bowing up as he seated himself fully. She wrapped her arms around his neck. "Please move."

"Yes, ma'am." He eased out before sliding back into place.

Mae gasped a little. "So accommodating."

He smiled against the skin of her neck. "I aim to please."

She hummed low and soft as he set a steady pace. "I guess we'll see." The smile on her lips slipped when he made sure his pelvis rocked against her on the next thrust. "Oh."

"Mm-hmm. Oh, is right." Boone tipped his head to catch a puckered barely-brown nipple in his mouth.

Every second that passed sent his focus deeper. Pulled him to that place that made it impossible to think of anything but her.

Her pleasure was his own need, and every sound she made fed that need, took it higher.

Mae's fingers dug into his skin like she hadn't already burrowed under it long ago, deep enough she was a part of him.

And now she was here.

She was his.

Again.

This time it would stay that way.

Her legs clenched at his hips as her pussy tightened around him, threatening to steal the last few seconds from him.

Boone opened his eyes, hoping for a last bit of focus to carry him through.

Instead he met her eyes.

And there was no more holding back.

No more focus.

There was only her.

She carried him over the edge and he went willingly.

It was all he'd ever wanted.

To be with her.

He'd follow her to the ends of the earth if that's what she wanted.

Whatever it took, however it had to happen.

He would never leave Mae Wells' side again.

———

BOONE LIFTED ONE lid, trying to figure out what woke him up from the soundest sleep he'd had in years.

The cabin was still dark. A few birds chirped outside the window, indicating his alarm would go off soon.

But not yet.

That meant something else cut his perfect night of sleep short.

Mae was draped across him, her body warm and heavy with sleep. She didn't budge as he leaned up to peer around the cabin, looking for the sleep-ending culprit.

A single creak was all the warning he got before the bed collapsed under them, hitting the floor with a loud crash, their bodies bouncing on the crappy mattress as it hit.

Mae's head popped up, hair over her face as she gripped him tight. "Boone?" Fear edged her voice and it brought him no small amount of satisfaction that he was the first thing she thought of.

He was who she knew would keep her safe.

"We broke the bed."

Mae swiped the hair off her face as she leaned to one side to look down at the destroyed frame. "I guess you can add *broke a bed* to your list of manly accomplishments."

He laughed as she wiggled off him, fighting to get loose

from the tangle of blankets. "Not sure it counts if it happens when you're sleeping."

Mae stole one of the blankets, wrapping it around her as she went toward the bathroom at the back of the cabin. "Good point. Guess you're back to being a non-bed breaker then." She shot him a little grin over one shoulder as she closed the door.

Boone sat up on the mattress, yawning as he scrubbed one hand down the back of his head.

"Hey."

He turned to find Mae peeking out the door at him.

"Go get a new bed." One finger came out to point at the bed. "That thing wasn't great even before it collapsed."

CHAPTER EIGHTEEN

MAE RELAXED IN the seat, head against the rest as the early morning air filtered in through the open windows.

Boone sat beside her, one hand on her thigh and the other slung over the wheel.

Music played softly through the speakers as he drove her home.

Mae rocked her head his direction, watching his profile in the dim light.

"Somethin' wrong?"

"I'm sorry I broke your bed."

"I'd say you put it out of its misery." He glanced her way, his expression relaxed. "That thing was awful."

"So why didn't you get a new one?"

"I've got other things I plan to spend my money on."

"Like?"

Boone faced forward, his eyes staying on the road. "Other things."

"That's very specific." She smiled a little. "Fine. Don't tell me."

"I don't plan to live my life alone, Mae." He kept his gaze straight ahead. "I still have all the same plans I had ten years ago."

"Not the same plans." She'd struggled to fall asleep last night and the horrible sleeping situation was only partly to blame. The rest of the reason had to do with figuring out where in the hell they went from here.

His eyes came her way. "How's that?"

"Unless you plan to get married right after graduation and start having babies right away then the plans aren't the same." She'd been so clueless at eighteen. So blind to how Boone might feel about all she hoped and dreamed to have.

Even a grown man could have folded under the pressure, let alone a nineteen-year-old kid.

"You have to update your plans." Mae glanced at the clock as they pulled into the back lot and parked.

"I have to update the timetable." Boone turned to her as he shut off the truck. "Not the plans."

"I guess we'll see." Mae opened her door and jumped out, turning to tell him goodbye.

But Boone was already out of the truck.

She lifted her brows. "Don't you have work to do?"

"Seems like I need to make sure you get some breakfast first." He stopped at the back of the truck and waited for her.

"I've got a ton to do this morning."

"Then it looks like I'm makin' breakfast." Boone stood close as she unlocked the deadbolt on the steel door leading to the kitchen. "'Cause I know for sure all you've had to eat since I picked you up yesterday is cobbler and ice cream."

"That's a decent dinner in my book."

"You gonna still think that when you're a momma and one of your kids is making the same argument?"

Mae's hand slipped off the key.

Motherhood wasn't anything she'd considered recently.

Not in years.

The Wooden Spoon became her baby.

She cleared her throat. "I guess I haven't thought much about it."

Boone's eyes stayed on her as she finished opening the door. Stepping into the space was an escape of sorts. A reminder that she'd made the most of the past ten years, even if they weren't what a naive girl expected them to be.

Boone was close behind her as she switched on the lights. "So if cobbler and ice cream is dinner what's breakfast?"

"Coffee." She went to one of the industrial makers and loaded the drip cup with her favorite breakfast blend before switching it on.

"I guess we're keepin' it simple then." He opened the cooler and pulled out four eggs from one of the flats, lifting them up as he went to where the pans were stashed. "Eggs and toast."

Mae sighed. The man was about to work a full morning on the ranch. No way would two eggs and a slice of bread be enough to sustain him. "You're kind of a pain in the ass, you know that?"

"Says the woman who broke my bed." He grinned at her across the counter between them.

"I didn't break your bed." Mae pulled out one of the thin-cut New York strips they used for their steak and egg breakfast, along with one of the containers of chunked potatoes they served alongside it.

"It was doin' just fine till you showed up."

She went to stand beside him, pulling out a large skillet that would hold the whole lot. "I know how it feels."

Boone leaned into her side as she clicked on the heat and added a swirl of oil and a pat of butter. "That because you're worried I'll break you?"

"No." The answer was easy. Not because she trusted Boone.

But because she knew herself well enough to know there wasn't anything that could break her.

Mae dropped the steak into the hot pan before scattering the precooked potatoes alongside. She peeked Boone's way. "But I had my life figured out." She scooted the potatoes around as the meat sizzled.

"That mean it's not so figured out now?" Boone snagged one of the bagged loaves of bread Carmen made the day before and pulled two pieces free.

"Honestly I don't know what it means." Mae cleared out a spot of the pan and added a little more butter before cracking in the eggs and popping on the lid. She rubbed her burning eyes. She'd hoped today to feel less complicated but so far that wasn't how it was turning out to be.

Realizing what she thought for the past ten years wasn't entirely accurate actually made some things more difficult to wrap her brain around.

And then there was the sex.

Which complicated everything all on its own.

Boone stepped in behind her, his hands resting on her shoulders. "Don't overthink it." He leaned down to press a kiss to the spot where her shoulder met her neck. "Just let it be what it is."

Mae tilted her head to glare at him. "Is that how this is going to be? You're going to use my words against me?" .

He smiled. "Absolutely."

———

MAE FELL TO the cushions of her couch.

She was freaking exhausted. Boone left after breakfast, giving her just enough time for a quick shower before the rest of the staff showed up and the day started.

Her head dropped back and she closed her eyes, intending to rest for just a second.

A melodic set of bells sent her sitting straight up thirty minutes later.

Mae snagged her cell phone and stared at the screen. It was an unfamiliar number. She contemplated ignoring it but ended up swiping across the screen at the last second. "Hello?"

"I thought you were going to leave me standing out here."

Mae stood up from the couch and walked into her bedroom. She separated two slats of the blind and peeked out into the back lot.

Sure enough, a cherry red truck was parked next to her SUV. "It would serve you right for just showing up here. She squinted down at his dark head. "Do you have a duffel bag?"

"Someone broke my bed."

"You have two." She backed away from the window and headed for the stairs.

"You saying we're sleeping at my place again?"

"I'm saying you're awful confident you're not sleeping alone tonight." She hit the bottom of the stairs and unlocked the door, pulling it open on Boone's smiling face.

He held up a large paper bag from Thomasino's. "I'm prepared to bribe my way in."

Mae groaned, grabbing the garlic-scented bag from him. "Damn it."

"Told you I've learned a thing or two." He grabbed her as she started to move away, pulling her in for a kiss. His lips lingered over hers. "I've got another bag too." He lifted the second bag. A carton of ice cream was visible through the plastic. "And there's lava cakes to go with them."

"You're awful."

"I'm smart." He kissed her again, this one quick and light. "Come on. I'm hungry." One hand rested on her back as they went up to her place, the scent of melted cheese and tomato sauce teasing her more with each passing second.

Mae went to the counter and opened the stapled bag, peering inside.

"I got lasagna and chicken Alfredo." Boone reached in to pull out two cardboard bowls with clear plastic lids. "And salads." He unloaded the rest of the food, which included two lava cakes dusted with powdered sugar.

Mae opened a drawer and pulled out two forks, handing one to Boone. He stacked the salads and entrees into a single tower and headed for the table.

"In this house we eat on the couch." Mae grabbed two bottles of water from the fridge and went to plop down on the sofa where she spent most of her evenings watching her guilty pleasures, shoving the antique wide cast iron baking tray she used as decoration out of the way. "While we watch television." She lifted a finger. "And don't ask me if I'll still say the same thing when I have kids."

"You still want to have kids?"

She shrugged. "I don't know. It's not really been anything I needed to think about."

Mae switched on the television, ready to take the conversation to a more comfortable place.

Boone looked at the screen then back at her, one dark brow lifted. "Interview with a Serial Killer?"

"Don't judge me." She settled into her spot, tray of lasagna on her lap. "It's interesting."

Boone chuckled as he eased down beside her. "I won't judge you over anything, Sweetheart. If it makes you happy, it makes me happy."

Mae tipped her eyes his way, fork between her lips. "I don't remember you being this agreeable."

"I probably wasn't." His body settled closer to hers. "I don't remember you being this forward with what you like."

"I probably wasn't." Mae let the revelation sit for a second. "I'm not sure I knew what I liked."

"Makes sense." Boone dug into the Alfredo. "We were pretty young."

Mae eyed him a little longer. "I'm sorry for making you feel pressured."

Boone's head snapped her way. "No." He shook his head. "You've got nothing to apologize for, Mae. Not a damn thing."

"I think you're wrong." It wasn't anything she would have said to him ten years ago. She was too insecure. Too immature. Too clueless about how things really worked to

217

feel comfortable putting her own thoughts out there. "I never asked how you felt. I never wondered if you were ready." She'd been so focused on herself and her life. "It doesn't mean I'm bad. I was just too young and didn't know it." Mae lifted one side of her mouth in a half smile. "Kinda like you."

Boone sucked in a breath, blowing it back out his nose as he stared at her. "I just want you to be happy."

"Isn't that what got you in trouble in the first place?" She lifted her shoulders. "Telling me what I wanted to hear even when you weren't sure?"

If they were going to do this again, then it had to be different. A fresh start built on a shared past that might give them a leg up.

Boone's blue eyes went over her shoulder toward the front windows she'd spent hours restoring. His brows pinched together. "Did you hear something?"

"It's just the cars on the street." It was one of the reasons she'd struggled to sleep last night. There were no sounds outside of the crickets and the occasional hoot of an owl. "The noise here is a lot different than it is on the ranch."

His eyes slowly came back her way. "You like it here?"

Living here was what made the most sense. She owned the building and there were two floors worth of space that needed using. "It's mine." Mae couldn't stifle the smile moving onto her lips. "And I have a king-sized bed that's not broken, so..."

"Rub it in." Boone set his container of pasta on the coffee table before stretching one arm across her shoulders. "You ready for cake and ice cream?"

Mae snapped the lid of her food in place. "I'm always ready for cake and ice cream."

Boone stood up and went to the kitchen, turning to look around. "Are you cooking something?"

Mae kicked her feet up on the table. "I cook all day. I don't cook at night."

He slowly turned in a circle. "It smells like something's cooking."

The words were barely out of his mouth when a piercing sound cut through the air. Boone's eyes met hers. "What is that?"

A chill ran down her spine.

She couldn't talk. Couldn't breathe.

A second later Mae saw the realization in his eyes.

Boone came rushing toward her, practically lifting her off the couch and dragging her to the door. He grabbed a towel off the stack sitting on the dryer and pressed it to her face before ripping the door open. The smoke was already in the stairwell, filling it with a grey stink. Making her eyes water and her skin itch.

Boone dragged her along, holding the towel in place as he pulled her down the stairs and to the back door.

Mae turned, the sight of the flames through the service window sending the food she'd just eaten climbing back up her throat. She tried to run toward it. Ready to fight for what she'd worked so hard to create, but Boone's hands held tight, refusing to let go. She screamed into the towel as he pulled her out the door and into the evening air.

Her feet didn't work but somehow she continued to move farther from the building she'd put her heart and soul into.

Her baby.

Boone's voice was ragged and rough as he spoke close to her ear.

But he wasn't talking to her.

"The sprinklers are on but it didn't look like they were gettin' it." Boone pulled her closer, wrapping one arm tight across her chest as he finally let the towel fall.

He coughed, the sound snapping her attention his way. "Are you okay?" She turned her back to the building as all her focus went to the man who put her safety above his own. Mae pressed her hands to his face as he leaned back against the side of his truck, cell phone pressed to his ear.

"She's okay." Boone pulled her against him, resting his head close to hers as sirens wailed in the distance. His other arm came around her, holding tight.

"Can you breathe okay?" Mae tried to see his face as she listened for any sign he might have inhaled too much smoke. "You should have covered your face too."

"There wasn't time." He straightened, pulling her along with him as the sirens became deafening, their wail bouncing off the buildings of downtown. His eyes were serious as they came to hers. "We need to go meet them at the front."

She nodded, wrapping one arm around his waist as they edged up the alley to the front of the building. Aside from the sound of the fire alarm and the faint smell of smoke there was no other sign anything was wrong.

Not until they reached the sidewalk.

One hand immediately went over her mouth.

The front window had a hole in the center. Cracks streaked out from the hole, but for the most part the window was still intact. Behind the busted glass flames licked along the wood furniture Carmen's husband made by hand for her.

Mae shook her head in disbelief. "What is happening?"

Fire was always a concern when you owned a restaurant. Accidental kitchen fires were something she tried to be prepared for.

But this wasn't a kitchen fire.

This also wasn't an accident.

Boone pulled her close as he looked up and down the street, his body angling to get between her and anyone who might be lingering. He pulled his phone out again, pressing it tight to his ear as the fire engines parked along the street and fully-geared men jumped from the doors.

"Grady?" His eyes went to Mae before moving to the hole in her window. "I think we've got a problem."

CHAPTER NINETEEN

HE WAS GOING to kill Junior Shepard.

Mae's eyes were wide as she stared at the glass that used to make up her front window. "Someone did this?"

"Grady is on his way with the fire marshall." Boone pulled her closer, the adrenaline in his veins making him need the connection as much as he expected she did. "We'll figure out what happened and get everything back the way it should be."

Mae's eyes lifted to the second floor. "What am I going to do?"

"Insurance will cover the repairs." He pressed his lips to the clammy skin of her forehead. "It'll be even better than new."

"But it's my business." Her hands came to the front of his shirt and held tight. "It's where I live."

"You can stay with me while everything is put back."

Mae's face crumpled. "You don't have a bed."

She was in shock and all he wanted to do was make it better somehow. "I'll buy any bed you want. You can pick it out." Boone smoothed down the back of her head with one hand as the firefighters knocked out the rest of the window and started hosing down the fire on the other side.

Mae pressed one hand to her forehead as she watched them dump gallon after gallon of water into the dining room. "I can't believe this is happening."

He should have seen it coming.

Should have known Junior wouldn't go down without a fight.

Should have done something to stop this before it happened.

A medic rushed their way. "You guys okay?"

One of the firefighters went for the front door with a battering ram. He slung it at the handmade door, rocking it on its hinges.

The second hit sent it splintering and Mae collapsing against him.

Boone caught her, scooping her up as she sagged toward the ground.

"Bring her over here." The medic led him through the crowd of people gathering from around town.

"What am I going to do?" Mae's head rolled to his shoulder.

He settled her onto the stretcher inside the ambulance and crouched down beside her as the medic checked her blood pressure. "You're going to take tonight to be upset about this, and then you're going to grab this by the balls and make it your bitch."

Mae's lips twitched a little. "Someone needs to cut off Junior's balls."

"Oh, Sweetheart, that's the least of what that son of a bitch has coming his way."

"Where is she?"

Boone turned to the open back doors just as his mother shoved her way through the crowd, his dad and Brooks right behind her.

Maryann didn't miss a beat as she pulled herself right up inside the ambulance. "Oh thank God." She shoved him over in her haste to reach Mae's side. She turned to Bill. "Call her momma and tell her Mae's okay." Maryann reached out to smooth one hand over Mae's forehead. "I was scared to death."

"I'm okay." Mae's eyes came his way before moving back to his mother. "How did my mom know?"

"They got a call from the company that monitors the alarms. When they couldn't reach you they called the back-up number. She called me because she knew I could get here faster." His mother's eyes went to the medic checking Mae over. "Everything's okay?"

"Her blood pressure just dropped a little bit. She's going to need to make sure she stays hydrated but other than that she's fine."

"Come on then. You don't need to stay to see this." His mother scooped Mae up turning to give him a look out of the side of her eye. "Help me get her out of here."

It was what he was planning on doing anyway, but letting his mother think it was her idea for him to help would serve him well. "Yes, ma'am."

Mae was a little more steady on her feet as she walked along with his mother toward the back lot where his truck was parked. Maryann loaded her into the passenger's side.

"You go on and get her set up in a room at The Inn. We'll handle things here."

"Yes, ma'am." Boone drove across the vacant land next to the lot instead of trying to fight his way through the mess on Main Street. The truck bounced a little as the tires went over the curb and onto the asphalt of the road.

He reached across the console to grab Mae's hand in his. One of her elbows was braced against the door and her head was resting in her hand.

There was not a thing he could or should say to her. Nothing could fix what happened. Nothing could make it better.

So he just had to be there for her.

Camille was on the porch of The Inn when they pulled up, waiting with Clara at her side. She ran down the steps toward Mae, grabbing her in a tight hug.

"I'm so sorry."

"None of this is your fault." Mae squeezed her friend back, her chin lifting as she took a deep breath. "It's all going to be fine. All of it can be replaced." Mae's eyes pinched shut as she and Camille continued to hold each other.

Finally Camille sucked in a breath and pulled away, clearing her throat. "I got a room ready for you." She peeked Boone's way. "One of the king suites."

Mae smiled a little. "Thank you."

Camille grabbed one of Mae's hands. "Thank *you*."

They stared at each other for a minute before turning toward where Clara stood on the porch, her expression hard.

Camille and Mae went inside but Clara caught him by the arm.

Her eyes watched as Mae and Camille went through the

front room of The Inn toward the kitchen at the back of the building. "Was it Junior?"

"Can't prove anything at this point." Boone kept his voice low in case Calvin was around. "But it seems like someone meant for this to happen."

Clara's nostrils flared. "Where do you think he is?"

"That is information I'm not giving you." He knew better than to disclose something like that to one of these women. He'd seen them face a man down with nothing but rolling pins and butcher knives. There was no telling what they'd do to Junior if they could find him.

Clara's lips flattened to a thin line as he walked past her and made his way to where Camille was scooping out a bowl of ice cream for Mae.

Mae sat on one of the stools lining the huge angled island. She frowned at him. "I didn't get to eat my lava cake."

"I'll buy you all the lava cakes you want." He stood at her side, one hand on her back.

She rested her head in her hand. "I need to call everyone and let them know what happened so they don't try to show up for work in the morning." She blinked a few times. "I need to call the insurance company." Her head fell back toward the vaulted ceiling. "Except I don't know anyone's freaking number."

Camille slid the bowl across to Mae along with a bottle of water. "I know their numbers. I'll call the staff." She pointed at the heap of chocolate, chocolate chip ice cream. "You eat that and breathe." Then she walked out the back door to pace around the pool, phone to her ear.

Clara slid into the stool on Mae's other side. "She's really upset."

"I know." Mae scooped in a little bite, putting the spoon in her mouth upside down. "She shouldn't be. None of this is her fault."

Clara's dark eyes rested on Mae. "I'm glad it was you he went after." She looked out to Camille. "I don't think she could handle it."

Mae sucked in a long breath. "He better not go after her."

"Maybe if someone would tell us where we could find him—"

"It's not happening." Boone tipped his head toward the front porch. "I'm gonna go make a couple calls, okay?"

Mae tipped her head in a nod.

He dialed Brooks as he went outside. His brother picked up on the second ring. "Hello."

"How's it look?" Boone fell into one of the chairs on the porch.

"Looks like most of the damage is in the dining room. Kitchen seems to be okay outside of the smoke. Upstairs is pretty untouched."

"The structure's okay?"

"Fire didn't get to much besides the front room and even there it didn't get deep." Brooks' voice muffled for a second before coming back. "Grady says they found what they think started it. Looks like someone threw a jar of gasoline through the window then found a way to light it up."

"Grady know where he is?"

"You know he's not going to tell any of us if he does." Brooks' tone softened. "Just stay there with Mae. Make sure she's okay. We'll get to handle this before long. There's no way Junior's going to be happy when he finds out the damage was minimal."

"All the more reason we should deal with this now instead of waiting."

"You already left her once, man. You think she'll be any happier if the next time you leave her is to go to jail?"

Boone straightened in the chair as he looked out over the fields. "Damn it, Brooks."

"That's what I thought." Brooks paused as their mother's voice carried on in the background. "Mom says she can go upstairs and get some things for Mae if that's okay."

"Let me go check." Boone went back inside and found Mae still sitting at the island. "Do you want my mom to get you anything from upstairs?"

Mae's slumped shoulders straightened. "They're letting her go up there?"

"Seems like."

"Can she get me some clothes?" Mae leaned forward. "And my phone?" Her lips pressed together.

"What else do you want, Sweetheart? She'll pack up the whole place if that's what you want."

A smile almost came on Mae's lips. "I'd really like to take a shower."

"Got it." Boone leaned in to press a kiss to her forehead before turning to head back outside. "You get all that?"

"She's already on her way. Sent Grady off to find her something to carry it all in."

"Camille's got Mae set up at The Inn."

"I'll bring it down so you don't have to deal with Mom."

"I appreciate it." Boone paused. "Thanks for doin' this."

"I'm hopin' you'll owe me one." His brother disconnected the line just as Mae stepped out onto the porch.

"Does this mean it's not bad?"

"Sounds like it's mostly the dining room and nothing really got to the actual building. Just what was inside it." Boone pulled her close, wrapping both arms around her as he rested his chin against the top of her head.

"Clara's right. I'm glad it was me and not Camille." She tipped her head back to look at him. "At least he knows better than to come out here."

"He's gonna know better than to even breathe in your direction soon."

"Hopefully they can charge him with this too." Mae rested her head against the center of his chest as she looked out over the ranch. "Whatever it takes to keep him away from Camille and Calvin."

She was so good. So strong. So sure of herself and what she was capable of.

A good friend. A good employer.

Somehow Mae managed to take something damn near perfect and improve on it.

Which had him wondering.

"Can I ask you something?"

"Only if I can ask you something back."

"Deal." She didn't have to bargain with him for answers. He'd tell her anything she wanted to know, anytime she wanted to know it. "Why is it none of the men I've heard tried to lock you down were successful?"

"Like who?"

"Grady for starters." The cop was salt of the earth. Good and honest and hardworking. The kind of man Mae should have fallen all over.

She shrugged. "I didn't really date anyone from town.

They all knew what happened with you and I was tired of talking about it all the time."

"I'm sorry I put that on you."

"You probably shouldn't be." She backed out of his arms toward the door. "If you hadn't I'd probably be married to Grady right now with five of his kids driving me crazy."

Boone's brows lifted. "Five?"

Mae rolled her eyes. "I just pulled that number out of the air."

He shook his head. "I don't know." Boone walked along, keeping up with her as she continued to back away. "It came out awful fast."

Mae's eyes widened. "I picked a number that was shockingly high."

"I'm not sure it's as shockingly high as you expected it to be."

Mae poked one finger his way. "Don't you put that evil on me, Boone Pace. One of you is hard enough to deal with."

"That sounded an awful lot like you're thinkin' of me as the father of your babies." He continued after her as she hit the stairs. "And now you're planning to give me all girls."

"That is *not* what I said." Mae sped up, taking the stairs a little faster. "You are putting words in my mouth."

"You're the one who said we were gonna have five daughters."

Mae scoffed. "I did not."

"That's what I heard." He grabbed her just as she reached the top of the stairs, grinning as she yelped. "But I guess four would be okay too."

She leaned into him as he walked her toward the first door on the left. It was half open where Camille left it ready for Mae. "I've got to get my first baby back where she should be before I can even think about something like that."

"I can call in some favors and have it done by the end of the month."

Mae sighed, turning in his arms to face him. "I need a little time, Boone."

Her comment sobered him. Knocked him back down where he should have been to start with. "I'm not tryin' to make you feel pressured, Mae. All this goes at your pace. I was just hopin' to lighten up the evening."

She smiled. "Thank you." Mae backed toward the large bed, snagging the remote off the mattress before switching on the television as she kicked off her shoes. She peeked over one shoulder. "Come on, Cowboy. Let's watch some television like normal people."

He glanced at the screen as she switched it to a channel. "Normal people don't watch how to kill other people."

"It's not a how-to show." Mae settled against the pillows. "It's a cautionary tale." She patted the bed beside her. "Come on."

Boone settled in beside her. The first episode was just wrapping up when there was a knock on the door.

Mae sat up straight. "Come in."

Camille came in with a large tub. "Here's the first one." Brooks said it had all your pajamas and toiletries in it."

Mae lifted the lid on the packed crate. "The first one?"

"There's three more." Camille smiled a little. "Apparently Maryann wanted to be sure you had everything you needed." Her smile faltered. "You okay?"

Mae gave Camille a genuine smile. "I am." She pulled out

a pair of sweatpants and a t-shirt. "Better now that I can get comfortable."

Camille dipped her head in a little nod. "If there's anything else you need just let me know." She gave Boone a little wave. "I'll see you guys in the morning."

Mae watched as Camille walked out the door, pulling it closed behind her. She turned to Boone, a look of resolution on her face. "Call Grady and make sure he does everything he can to prove Junior did this." One finger pointed to the television. "'Cause I can promise you they won't be making a show about me." Her lips pulled into a smile that would scare most men. "Because I definitely won't be getting caught."

CHAPTER TWENTY

MAE STOOD UNDER the hot water, washing the charcoal broiled smell out of her hair.

This shower was going to be the official end of her short-lived pity party. There wasn't time for her to wallow and she sure as hell wasn't going to put that on Camille.

Which is what would most certainly happen if she wasn't careful.

That meant from this point forward she was fine.

Everything was fine.

Except the part where Boone wanted five daughters.

Mae toweled off, wiping down with her favorite scented lotion before having at her hair with the dryer. By the time she was pajama-d up she felt a hundred times better about everything.

Except the part where Boone wanted five daughters.

Mae opened the door and found the room empty.

Which was more than a little disappointing.

She walked into the suite and stared at the empty bed.

"You look upset."

Boone's deep voice sent her spinning toward the door. His hair was still damp and he was breathing a little heavy.

"Where did you go?"

"Went to take a shower of my own." He closed the door and flipped the lock before going to the table in the corner and setting down a small duffel bag. "Thought for sure I could beat you back."

"You thought wrong." She crossed her arms over her chest. "And I don't want to have five babies."

His brows went up. "I thought you hadn't thought about it."

"I haven't." She dropped her arms. "I'm just saying."

"That's understandable." Boone slowly came her way. "Four's plenty."

Mae huffed out a breath. "I don't want to talk about babies."

"You're the one who brought it up this time, Sweetheart." His smile was slow and easy. "Not me."

"You started it, though." She stood tall as he came in close. "With all your putting words in my mouth earlier."

"Thought you didn't want to talk about it."

"I don't." She didn't.

"So we won't then." Boone reached up to grab a bit of her hair. "I haven't seen you with your hair down in a long time."

"My hair was down the night I got a flat tire." How was that only a week ago?

"You were soaked that night." His eyes drifted down her front. "That dress was plastered to you."

"Are you only here because I look good hosed down?"

"It's one of the main reasons." He smiled. "I also like your pie."

"No—" She held her finger up between them. "Don't you dare. You will get no pie ever again."

Boone suddenly grabbed her, hefting her off the ground and dropping her into the middle of the mattress before crawling over her. "You've got a lot of rules when it comes to pie." He grabbed the sweats she'd been so happy to put on and yanked hard, pulling the baggy pants down her legs in one quick move. He lifted a brow at her panties.

"Shut up." Mae kicked at him.

"Looks like you were expecting these to be seen, Sweetheart." He reached up to run one finger down the center of the pink lace hip huggers.

"You've never taken the time to look at my panties. Maybe I wear these all the time."

A low hum rumbled through Boone's chest. "That might be the best news I've heard all day." His finger moved over the arc of her mound, tracing the line of her pussy. "Gives me something to look forward to every night."

Well shit.

Now she had to go buy more panties like this so he didn't catch onto her fib.

His finger hooked into the bit of fabric between her legs, tugging it to one side. The other hand palmed her thigh, pushing it open as his thumb stroked the bit of her he'd exposed, spreading her apart. Boone's head dropped to where his thumb held her open for his tongue and lips. She gasped when the heat of his mouth closed around her, teasing the only bit of her not still covered by the panties she still wore.

His tongue stroked against her clit as his hand pressed her thigh wider, making room for his broad shoulders as he settled between her legs. The second she started to edge toward climax he would shift gears, changing the movement and the speed, slowing her down before building her back up.

And then he would do it again.

"Boone. Don't do this to me." Mae grabbed at his hair but he dodged her.

"You're going to have to get used to this, Sweetheart because I don't plan to ever *not* do this to you." He pushed up, letting her panties snap back into place. "Especially if you're gonna lie to me about the panties you wear." He wiped across his mouth with one forearm, eyes dark. "Take your shirt off."

She blinked up at him. "What?"

"You heard me." He dug into the pocket of his athletic pants, pulling out a condom. "Take it off."

The roughness in his voice was doing something for her, and that was before she even considered the ragged demand that came with it.

"I'll take my shirt off if you take yours off first."

Boone smirked down at her. "Careful. I'll think you just want me for my body."

"Maybe I do."

He immediately grabbed the back of his shirt and tugged it up and over, tossing it to the ground before tipping his head her way. "Your turn."

The way he watched made it impossible to look away from his face.

It was as if he couldn't stand to wait any longer.

Like he didn't want to blink because he would miss a second of her skin.

Mae pinched the hem of the t-shirt between her fingers and slowly lifted it up over her belly.

She had to arch her back and wiggle a little to work it the rest of the way off.

"Christ." Boone's body dropped to hers while the shirt was still caught on her shoulders and head, his mouth catching a nipple and making the task infinitely more difficult than it should have been.

His hands gripped the fabric, helping her work it off as his tongue teased the opposite nipple, flicking it until it was painfully tight before sucking it into the heat of his mouth. He growled against her skin. "That fucking wiggle did me in." Boone pushed up to his knees and shoved his pants down to his thighs.

Mae held his eyes as she did it again, moving her hips and shoulders in a little rolling motion.

"You're going to kill me with that." Boone ripped open the condom in his hand.

"Maybe that's what I'm hoping for."

Boone rolled the condom down his length before yanking her panties to one side like he did before. "Be careful what you wish for, Sweetheart." The head of his dick pressed against her almost immediately, easing into her with a steady glide that sucked the air from her lungs. His body fell to hers as he seated himself fully, rocking against her. He stretched the lace farther, pressing his thumb to her clit.

"Oh—"

The sound was cut short as his hand clamped down on her mouth. Boone's lips moved along her neck as he continued to press into her with a perfect pace. "Gotta be quiet here, Sweetheart."

Mae nodded her head, squeezing her eyes shut as his thumb continued rubbing in time with the thrust of his hips.

Boone's mouth moved down, finding a nipple.

Mae flipped a pillow over her face and pressed it tight.

A second later it whipped away. "No way I'm not looking at your face while you come for me."

Her legs jerked.

Boone's mouth covered hers, smothering out the sound she tried unsuccessfully to contain.

For all she knew he might have been just as unsuccessful at it. All she could hear was the ringing in her ears as the press of his thumb and the pressure of his cock worked in perfect harmony to steal her senses, leaving her with nothing but where he touched her.

Where he kissed her.

Where he filled her.

Her whole body went stiff, clenching as she came, holding him tight as everything that used to matter just stopped.

Boone moved a little faster. A little harder.

A little rougher.

His body shifted, hips angling in a different way as he chased what he'd just given her.

"I love you, Mae. I never stopped." His words were choppy from where his face was pressed to the skin of her neck. "You're it for me. You're all of it."

Whether it was the change in what he was doing or the words coming out of his mouth, a heat deep in her core flared to life, blazing higher with each slam of his body into hers. She arched her back, chasing the feeling she couldn't explain, trying desperately to find it.

Boone shifted again, this time picking up her leg and holding it high before bracing her other thigh between his in a move that rolled her almost to her side.

And it changed everything.

Mae pressed both hands over her mouth as he raked over the spot he'd barely been teasing a second ago. Now each move he made dragged against it, stimulating her in a way that made her toes curl and her back bow.

"That's it." Boone's voice was low and rough in her ear. "Give me one more, Mae. Come with me."

The swell of his dick was all it took, the extra pressure just enough to send her over the edge a second time.

It was a damn miracle.

One that drained every bit of energy she had left.

Her arms flopped to the mattress as she stared at the ceiling.

Blinking.

Boone collapsed beside her, his breathing still ragged as he pressed a kiss to her temple. "Still think I'm amateurish?"

———

"YOU FEEL BETTER now that you've seen it?" Boone opened the door to the truck and stayed close while she slid out.

"I mean, it still sucks but it could have been worse." They'd spent the whole morning meeting with the insurance adjuster, going over the police report and the damage done. "At least we can get started quickly." The damage was all cosmetic, and most of it was actually from the water they used to put out the fire itself.

"I think we need to be thoughtful about this." Boone was

really quiet through all of it, spending most of his time talking to Grady while she went over her policy information and procedures with the insurance adjuster.

"What do you mean?" She was ready to get her people back to work. Get back in her home. The Inn was nice, but staying there long-term was nothing she was interested in doing.

Boone huffed out a sigh. "I mean we need to make sure the place is secure before you get to putting it back together again."

It was the part of this she was trying really hard not to think about. "He's probably done."

"That's not how this works, Sweetheart. Men like Junior don't give up easy. It's why Camille stayed as long as she did. She knew it would be like this."

Mae glanced toward The Inn. "I thought Grady said they might be able to prove it was him."

Boone kicked at a pile of gravel. "Seems like that might not be as easy as he initially thought."

Mae smoothed down her hair as the wind blew it across her face. "I can't just wait around forever."

"Doesn't have to be forever." Boone took her hand in his. "Just until someone can figure out a way to make sure Junior behaves himself."

Mae followed along as he led her toward the barn. "Someone?"

Boone shrugged. "I'm sure there's a few people lookin' to chat with him."

"Chat." Mae had a front row seat to the teenage years that earned the Pace boys their reputation.

She knew what *chat* meant.

"If I can't hunt him down, you can't hunt him down either."

"You want to take a ride with me?" Boone led her through the doors and into the barn near the cabins.

"I feel like you're changing the subject."

"You didn't answer my question."

"Please don't get into trouble." The thought roused an old ache in her chest, making her feel even more emotional than she'd been seeing the destruction done to her restaurant. "Please."

Boone's face became serious. "I don't plan to leave you again for any reason, Mae. Definitely not because of a prick like Junior."

She believed him.

Mostly.

Boone stopped at one of the stalls. "Now, how about you pick a horse so we can get going?"

"Not Nellie. She's a traitor." Mae peeked over the gate at the horse in the stall where Boone stopped. "Who's this?"

"That's Baron."

"Fancy." Mae leaned back as the gelding came to the gate, reaching his head over the top to sniff her gently.

"He's real calm." Boone stroked down the horse's sleek black neck. "I think you two will get along."

Mae looked up at the horse. "Looks like you and I get to take a ride, Baron."

Boone seemed to have everything ready for the ride, including the horse stashed in the barn with Nellie. They were the only two still stalled up, which meant this trip was planned.

Boone finished checking Baron's saddle before turning to her. "He's ready for you."

"He's bigger than Nellie."

"He's a big baby though." Boone patted the horse's rump. "I wouldn't put you on a horse I didn't trust completely." He stood by as she saddled up and settled into the seat. "You good?"

She checked the length of the stirrups, making sure everything was in an okay spot. "I think so."

"Let's go then." Boone was up and on Nellie in the blink of an eye. The smaller mare led the way, taking them across fields in a direction that was oddly familiar.

Then again, most of the ranch looked the same. Fields. Fences. Pastures.

Cows.

It wasn't until she saw the copse of trees that Mae realized exactly where they were going.

The part of the ranch she thought of more than she should.

Boone and Nellie went straight into the trees, moving toward the center where a tall tree stood, its top branches peeking out above all the others around it.

It was a tree she remembered as being strong and green and lush.

"What's wrong with the tree?"

"It's got Oak Wilt." Boone swung to the ground before coming to Baron's side as she did the same.

"Will it be okay?" Mae glanced down at the browned leaves covering the ground.

"I've treated it but it's not getting any better." Boone

stayed put as she walked to the trunk, resting her hand on the bark.

"Is it going to die?" Mae circled the wide base, keeping her hand on the rough surface as she went, not stopping until she found what she was looking for.

Sort of.

She let her fingers move into the grooves Boone etched with his pocket knife over a decade ago.

BP+MW

Some of the bark had fallen away, revealing the cuts that were deep enough to hit the wood itself. She traced each letter. "I remember when you did this."

"It was the night I told you I loved you."

She'd believed him then. Knew in her heart and soul it was the truth.

For ten years she thought it was a lie she'd been stupid enough to believe.

A lie she never really knew how to get past.

Because maybe it wasn't really a lie at all.

CHAPTER TWENTY-ONE

"IT WAS ALREADY sick when I came back." Boone rested one hand on the tree he'd tried to save. "I hoped I could bring it back."

"Sometimes things are already too far gone by the time you try to save them." Mae's eyes slid his way. "Doesn't matter what you do."

He knew they weren't quite on the same page, but after last night he hoped they were at least in the same book. "You trying to tell me something?"

"Some things can be brought back and some can't." Mae traced their initials with the tip of one finger. "Sometimes it's best to just let go."

"Is that what you want to do? Just let go?"

Mae tipped her head back to look up at the naked branches of the tree. "I think that's what we have to do."

"So what now?"

Mae's eyes went back to where he'd so painstakingly carved their forever into the tree, not knowing the path to get there would be so corroded.

And possibly ending.

"I hate the thought of it just decaying out here." Mae turned to him. "You could cut it down and have it milled." She looked to their initials. "Except this part. I think we should save this." She smiled as she stroked over the etched wood. "Maybe do something with it someday."

"You want to cut the tree down." Relief and hope tried to edge their way in. "And do what with it?"

Mae shrugged.

Like she didn't already have an idea.

"You could use it for all sorts of things." She shrugged again and continued to creep around the edges of what she was saying. "Oak makes beautiful furniture."

"It's sturdy." Boone followed her as she moved away from their tree. The tree he thought of as a symbol of what they were and could be. "Lasts forever."

"If you take care of it." Mae peeked at him over one shoulder, her eyes holding his a second before skimming to the branches. "Just because it can't be a tree anymore doesn't mean it can't be something just as beautiful."

As a kid he'd been too stupid to see her way of sharing what she thought. How she felt. "I love you, Mae."

Mae moved through the trees toward the edge of the cluster, stepping out into the sun. "I know." She turned his way. "Tell me what you think of when you're out here."

"The truth?"

Her lips rolled together as if she was preparing for something she knew might be too much. "The truth."

"Us." Boone looked out over the space he'd earmarked as his own years ago.

"We spent a lot of time out here."

He shook his head. "I don't think of us back then when I'm out here." Boone reached for her, pulling Mae close. "I think of us now. The us that's coming."

He paused, uncertain if he should keep going.

Mae's eyes were on him, waiting.

"This spot is mine. Where I want to build my house. Where I want my kids to play."

"All four of them?"

The fear she would be overwhelmed by all he wanted eased. "I believe it was five." Boone lifted his brows. "Girls, since you're worried about boys being a handful."

"I'm not sure it will matter." Mae almost smiled. "I've met your nieces, remember?"

"That mean I get boys and girls?"

"Pretty sure that's not how it works." Mae did smile now. "You get what you get."

"All boys. All girls. Boys and girls. Doesn't matter to me." He reached up to drag his thumb across her cheek. "All that matters to me is that you're the one going through it with me."

Mae looked at him for a few long heartbeats. "I'm open to considering the possibility."

Every cell of his body seemed to let out a breath of relief. "That's more than I could hope for."

"I don't know about that." Mae's lips twisted to one side. "I've heard I'm too focused on my career."

"No one woulda said that to you if you had a dick, Sweetheart. Means it's a lie said by a man with plenty of room in his blue jeans."

Mae gave him a one-sided smile. "I'm going to go with

that as the reason." She rolled her eyes toward the sky. "He did have little-dick energy."

Boone's head fell back on a laugh. "Haven't heard that, but it's a hell of a way to describe an asshole."

"It's a pretty common phrase in the female population." Mae leaned into him, resting her head against his chest. "I'm sorry our tree got sick."

Boone rested his lips against the top of her head. "I'm sorry I couldn't save it."

"There's only so much you can do." Her head turned to look in the opposite direction. "Is this really where you want to live?"

"It's already been surveyed."

Mae's head tipped back, her eyes coming his way. "Tired of living in the cabin?"

"Well, someone broke my bed so I had to do something."

"A bed breaks and your plan is to just go build a new house?"

"My motives are a little prettier than that." He picked her up and spun her around. "Come on. We should get back."

"Deflection." Mae smiled at him as he set her back on her feet. "Smart."

"I'm a smart guy." Boone slid his hand into hers as they walked back toward the horses. "I did figure out how to make the prettiest girl in town like me." He glanced Mae's way. "Twice."

"I don't know about prettiest." Mae continued smiling as they crossed the space where a house would soon be.

"I do." Boone stood at Baron's side as Mae lifted up into the saddle. "And I'll fight anyone who says different."

"I'm one hundred percent sure Brody is positive he has the prettiest girl in town."

"That's probably a good thing." Boone saddled up and Nellie immediately started toward the cabins. "But he's still wrong."

Mae laughed as she rode beside him. Baron put her sitting taller so she could see anything she wanted. Her eyes moved the whole trip back, making it clear his choice was the right one. They got back, handled the tack and set the horses out to graze in the fenced pasture at the back of the barn.

Mae watched as Baron and Nellie stuck together, looking for a bit of overgrown grass to chew.

"I thought you would like him."

"He seems to like Nellie." Mae leaned her arms over the fence rail.

"He's sweet on her for sure. Would follow her to the end of the earth."

"That why you picked him for me? So I'd have to follow you wherever you go?"

Boone turned to Mae. "Sweetheart, on that horse is the only time you will ever be the one following in this relationship."

"Is that what this is? A relationship?"

"For now." Boone stepped in close. "Until I can figure out how to convince you to let it be more."

"You have a plan for that?"

"Absolutely I do." He stepped away from the fence, holding one hand out to her. "It includes lots of ice cream."

Mae took his hand. "I should be mad at Camille for spilling my secrets."

"Or you should thank her." Boone fell in beside Mae as they walked to his truck. "Now you get all the ice cream I can manage to fit in a freezer." He opened the passenger's door and waited as Mae climbed in, claiming the space that was hers from the first time she sat in it, soaking wet and mad as hell.

They drove to The Inn where a number of cars were parked outside, including Mae's. They'd brought it back this morning after they finished with the adjuster. "Looks like there's a party."

Mae squinted at a small four-door hatchback. "Looks like Nora's here."

"Nora the new interior decorator?"

"Yeah." Mae glanced his way. "She might sort of hate your guts."

"Understandable." Boone grinned her way. "I hear I've been known to make stupid decisions."

Mae didn't smile back. "Not being ready for something doesn't make you stupid."

"Running away like a coward does." Boone leaned over to press a kiss to her lips. "And I'm man enough to own that." He jumped out of the truck and went to meet Mae on her side. "I'll let you spend time with them. I should go check in with my brothers."

Mae eyed him. "When you say check in…"

"We've got a ranch to run, Sweetheart." He leaned down to catch her lips in another kiss. "*Check in* means get to work."

Mae's eyes narrowed as they lingered on his face. "I feel like I don't believe that's what it means today."

It was sort of what it meant today. There was plenty of work to be done and all of it started and ended in one place.

Wherever Junior Shepard was hiding.

"I've got responsibilities, Mae. More and more every day." He was working hard not to lie to her. They did have a ranch to run.

He did have responsibilities.

She was one of them.

The most important one.

"Don't do anything stupid."

"I have no intention of doing anything stupid." Finding Junior was the smartest thing he could think of doing.

Mae's lips flattened. "Don't go find Junior."

"I'm not sure Junior's findable. He's probably working real hard to make himself scarce."

"You know he's not that smart, Boone."

Boone smiled because that's exactly what he was banking on. "I won't lay a finger on Junior. How's that?"

Mae's suspicious gaze held a second longer before she finally seemed appeased. "Good."

He tipped his head toward The Inn. "Go spend some time with your friends. I'm sure they want to see that you're okay."

Mae poked him in the center of the chest. "Don't get in trouble."

That was an easier thing to promise. "I won't."

He had no intention of doing anything that might get him in trouble. Derail all the plans he could finally put into motion.

Boone watched as Mae walked to The Inn. He smiled as

she peeked back at him before going inside, poking her finger his way with a glare before disappearing into the building.

He called Brody as he pulled down the gravel drive. "Where is everyone?"

"We're at Brooks and Brett's place. You comin'?"

"On my way." A couple minutes later he was parking in the line of trucks and heading inside where his brothers were situated around the front room.

"Y'all talking about what I think you're talkin' about?" Boone dropped to one of the recliners.

"We gotta deal with Junior." Brett was leaned against the edge of the counter in the open kitchen. "As long as he's running around Camille and Calvin aren't safe."

"Or Mae." Brooks sat in the other recliner, rocking a little. "Hell, he might go after any one of us at this point."

"Let him come." Boone relaxed back in the seat. "If he comes here then we got no problems. We can handle it with no issues."

"If he comes here then there's the chance Cal will see something, and he's seen enough already." Brett's jaw was tight. "We need to go to him."

"That would be fine except no one knows where the bastard is." Boone spent the morning talking to Grady and the information available was slim. "Grady said they haven't had a single lead on where he might be staying."

"Grady's gonna say that." Brett straightened. "He knows damn well what'll happen if we find out where Junior is." He dug his keys from the pocket of his worn jeans. "I say we go hunting."

Boone looked from brother to brother. "Been a long time since we went hunting."

They'd spent high school dishing out teenage vigilante justice. Putting the bad seeds of Moss Creek into their place.

"I think it's high time Junior Shepard gets what's comin' to him." Brett was already at the door. "Anyone comin' with me?"

Brooks stood with Boone a close second. Brody crossed the room to take the keys from Brett. "I'm drivin'."

Brett smiled. "Leaves my hands free."

They piled into Brett's truck, all four of them filling the extended cab. Their first stop was obvious.

"What in *the* hell." Brett leaned out the passenger's window as they pulled up in front of Junior's house.

The yard was littered with everything from clothing to furniture to appliances.

"Looks like baby threw a tantrum." Brody parked the truck, leaving the engine running as he climbed out.

Boone walked toward the house, scanning the items strewn across the patchy grass. "It's all Camille's stuff." Dresses, makeup, and curling irons were ripped, broken, and mangled. Destroyed and left out as evidence of how unhinged Junior really was. He looked up at the porch. "Front door's open."

Brett was the first one there, marching straight inside.

Boone went in behind him. "Holy hell." He pushed his arm under his nose. "What is that?"

"Hopefully Junior's dead body." Brett went to the back bedrooms, looking in both before flipping the switch in the bathroom.

Nothing happened.

"Power's off." Brett came through the living room,

heading to the kitchen. He stood staring into the space. "This explains the smell."

Boone stopped at the doorway. Cabinets were open and emptied, their contents spilled across the floor. Boxes of cereal and pasta were dumped out, but it was difficult to tell if it was Junior's doing or the animals who'd clearly been inside. The fridge was tipped, doors ajar, everything inside rotting across the floor where bugs stuck in the muck and mess.

"What in the hell is wrong with him?" Brody stood just behind Boone with Brooks at his side.

"I'm not sure we have time to go over that list." Boone scanned the tiny house. "But it looks like he's not here."

"Next stop is his momma's house." Brett pushed past them, headed straight for the front door.

Brody turned as Brett walked past. "You really want to go knocking on his parents' door?"

"Not planning to stop in for a chat." Brett paused on the porch. "I plan to hunt him down like the dog he is and take what he owes Camille out of his hide."

"He's not worth enough to get all that back." Boone followed Brett outside. "Once we find him we should call Grady. Let them handle it."

Brett spun his way. "How'd that work out last time?" He shook his head. "I'm not giving him the chance to come after Camille and Calvin. It's not fucking happening. I'll sit in jail to make sure of it."

In high school they would have all been on the same page. All for one and one for all.

Now things were different. More was on the line. "Brody

will be just as guilty as you are, Brett. We're all in this together and we'll all fall together if we're not careful."

Brett paced along the dirt drive. "So what in the hell are we supposed to do? Just let him keep fucking breathing until he manages to hurt one of them enough that Grady can actually do something?"

"We keep them safe. That's what we do." Boone kept his tone calm. "They're all with us now. We can make sure he can't get to them."

Brett's eyes came to his, holding steady with a simmering rage he'd never seen from his normally easy-going brother. "Calvin's got to go to school."

They all went silent.

This wasn't just about keeping Camille safe.

Or even Mae.

There was a little boy on the line. One who'd already been through too much in his short life.

Brody tipped his head. "Let's go find the son of a bitch then."

CHAPTER TWENTY-TWO

"HOW'S YOUR DAY been?" Camille looked up from where she stood at the counter and gave Mae a little smile as she walked into the kitchen at The Inn.

"It's been good." Mae slid onto a stool. "Really good actually."

Clara lifted her brows. "Really good?" She grinned. "Can I tell you a secret?"

"Does it involve Brody's bedroom skills again?"

"Not this time." Clara scooted closer. "I was really hoping you and Boone might figure things out because I really wanted you in my corner at family get-togethers."

"They are a lot, aren't they?" Nora's eyes widened as they snapped to where Clara and Mae sat. "Not that it's a bad thing." She looked a little panicked. "It's just," she looked toward Camille, "they're a lot sometimes."

"They are a lot most of the time." Clara wrapped one arm around Mae. That's why I'm glad I won't be the only one who feels like a deer in the headlights."

"It'll be better once your house is finished." Camille

worked her way around the kitchen, organizing the groceries Maryann delivered this morning before going back to the main house. "Then you will have your own space."

"It's not even that." Clara shrugged. "I've just never been around anyone like them. It's not a bad thing, it's just so different that sometimes I don't know how to act."

"There's people everywhere all the time." Nora peeked down into the mug in front of her. "I don't see how they deal with it."

"You get used to that part really fast." Clara leaned back in her seat. "For me it's having someone else there to do the things I've always done." Her lips fell into a serious line. "I feel guilty when it's not me doing them."

Camille snorted. "I completely understand that." She hefted out a sigh. "And how do you repay something like that?"

"I mean, I'm marrying their son, so..." Clara rolled her eyes Mae's way. "That's one way."

Mae held one hand up. "Not there yet."

Clara shrugged. "Can't blame me for trying."

Mae blinked a few times, trying to clear something stuck in her eye.

Camille leaned across the counter. "You okay?"

"I think I have something in my eye. Probably straw. I'll be right back." Mae went to one of the half-baths stationed around the main floor of The Inn and flipped on the light. She leaned into the mirror, blinking as she tried to see what might be caught. Unfortunately it wasn't a foreign object.

It was her darn contact.

"Shit." She pulled it free and peered down at it with her good eye. The soft lens was torn along one edge, leaving a strip flapping around. Mae flicked it in the trash before going back out to the kitchen. "My contact tore."

Clara spun in her seat. "You gonna go put another one in? We won't talk about anything interesting while you're gone."

"I don't have any more here." She covered her naked eye with one hand as it tried desperately to find focus. "I wish this happened earlier. I could have grabbed a spare while I was in town this morning."

"Let's go get them now." Clara jumped off her stool. "Then maybe we can go shopping or something."

"It's weird to have babysitters, right?" Camille looked around the quiet space. "And to have time to yourself."

"That's also pretty easy to get used to." Clara was essentially a single mother long before she separated from Wyatt's father. For the first time in her life she had a support system and it was amazing to watch her blossom and find herself.

"I could use a new pair of hiking boots." Mae glanced toward Nora and Camille. "You guys interested?"

"In going somewhere populated?" Nora practically leapt from her seat. "Hell yes."

Camille was the only one to hesitate. "I should stay here. Keep an eye on things."

"No one expects you to work around the clock, Camille." Clara sighed. "And if they think you're not taking enough time for yourself they will absolutely figure out ways to force it on you, so you might as well just do it."

Camille rocked on her feet. "We won't be gone too long, right?"

Clara had one hand tucked behind her back, fingers crossed. "Definitely not."

Camille gave a little nod. "Okay."

The women went outside and stared down the line of cars. Mae's was the only one well-suited to handle all four of them.

Mae turned to Clara. "You want to drive my car into town? I can't really drive with one contact in."

"I would love to drive." Clara took the keys and climbed into the driver's seat. She ran her hands over the wheel. "Fancy."

"Not fancy. Just new." Mae buckled into the passenger's seat, squinting one eye closed. "You could probably use a new car since you're hauling the girls around."

"Brody's been talking about it, but I hate the idea of spending money on something like that when my car still works perfectly fine." Clara started the engine and carefully backed out and headed down the driveway. "It's hard to get over the fear of not having enough money to take care of your kids."

"Do you think you'll ever get over it?" Camille's voice was quiet from where she sat in the back seat.

"I doubt it." Clara's expression was sad. "I just hope Wyatt doesn't still have the same worries he used to have."

Camille's chin dipped as she looked out the window.

Clara took a deep breath and smiled. The expression was tight and uncomfortable looking. "Where do you want to go, Nora?"

"Anywhere with more than five people." The interior decorator Maryann brought in to help with The Inn was staying in town temporarily while they finished putting things together, and it was clear she was missing the faster paced life she lived outside of Moss Creek. "Is there a mall? Maybe a shopping center that isn't just a row of shops?"

"We could go to Billings." Mae turned to look at Nora with her good eye. "There's a lot there."

"I think we have different definitions of a lot."

"That's what happens when you grow up someplace glamorous." Mae faced forward and closed both her lids, trying to reduce the strain on her eyeballs. "Not that I don't plan to come visit you when you go back home."

"I've got to find a new apartment first." Nora's frown was obvious even without seeing it. "Unless you feel like hanging out in a storage unit full of half-assedly packed stuff."

"I'm going to have to find out a way to use that word in a conversation." Mae turned toward Clara. "Not in front of the girls. I don't want to get on Maryann's bad side right out of the gate."

"I think we're immune from her bad side." Clara smiled her way. "Especially you. She'll be extra nice to you so she doesn't spook you."

Mae closed her eyes again. "I missed her."

"She missed you." Clara pulled to a stop at the front of The Wooden Spoon. "That's why she was so mad at Boone. She loved you and he took you away from her."

She'd spent years avoiding Maryann like the plague. Seeing her reminded Mae of all she believed she'd lost out on.

It took coming out the other end to realize she hadn't actually lost anything.

But she'd gained a hell of a lot.

Mae grabbed the keys to the building from the center console and pushed open her door. "I'll be right back."

"You don't want us to come in with you?" Clara had one hand on the ignition.

"The insurance guy said I shouldn't let anyone in until it's been inspected by the city." She closed the door. "It will only take me a second." Mae turned and went to the front door, doing her best to avoid looking at the giant panel of plywood where her beautiful front window used to be.

And would be again.

This is what she'd gained while Boone was gone.

The ability to take care of herself in every sense. Financially. Emotionally.

She was built of sturdier stuff than she would have known if he'd stayed and given her the life she thought she wanted.

Mae opened the newly-hung steel door temporarily serving as the front entrance, and went inside. Large fans were running, along with a number of industrial-sized dehumidifiers. It was the first thing they'd done once an electrician cleared them to hook up. Hopefully they caught it soon enough to make sure there wasn't any mold growth, because that would change everything.

The tables Carmen's husband made were destroyed, along with most of the booths and the drink station.

But all of that could be replaced.

Everything could be put back the way it was supposed to be and this time she would have it all. The restaurant she loved.

The man she might also love.

Would she have known something was missing if Boone had stayed all those years ago? Would she have realized she'd settled?

Not for the man.

For the life.

Would she have longed for something of her own? An identity outside of being the wife and mother she thought was all she could want?

Probably.

Mae went past the back door and started up the stairs Boone dragged her down, putting her safety ahead of his own. She smiled, running one hand along the wall grayed out with ash and soot.

For the first time she felt like everything was what it should be. In spite of the fire.

She hadn't really missed out on anything. She hadn't lost.

She'd gained.

And so had Boone.

Neither of them would ever wonder or regret.

The door to her apartment was ajar. Probably from the insurance adjuster making his assessments this morning.

She pushed it wide and stepped into the laundry room, her eyes going to the stack of towels sitting there, the top one missing.

Mae was still smiling as she went into the main room, ready to grab some contacts and get on with her life.

A life she built and chose.

Her smile faltered and her steps stopped.

The kitchen was ransacked. Food was spilled everywhere. Milk poured from the carton. Juice on the carpet.

Her couch was sliced open, stuffing pulled out and thrown everywhere. Her television screen was smashed.

Everything was destroyed. Broken. Bashed. Slashed.

"Well lookie who we have here."

A chill clawed down her spine at the voice coming from her bedroom doorway.

Mae spun to face the man who caused all the destruction. The man who was trying to destroy her for destroying him. "Get out of my house, Junior."

"Not in a place to make threats, Miss Mae." His pudgy frame moved into the small hall, revealing the pistol in his hand.

"You shouldn't be here."

"You fucked up my life." He grinned. "Now I'm fucking yours up back."

Junior's skin was ruddy. His eyes glassy and blurred. He was clearly drunk.

And pointing a gun right at her.

"Well you succeeded." She backed away as he came closer, keeping her eyes on him as she scrambled to come up with something she could use as a weapon.

"Not hardly." He reached up to shove the end of one finger into a nostril, digging it around before squinting down at it.

Then the bastard wiped his fucking booger on her counter.

"You see," Junior continued to advance on her, "you're the reason I ain't got no wife. It seems only fitting I figure out how to make sure you ain't got no husband."

"Well I beat you to that one." She sidestepped as he closed in, circling the coffee table covered in billowy white stuffing. "Because I don't have a husband."

"You got a man loves you enough to try to be." Junior's

eyes pinned hers and a grin that was almost a snarl curled his lips. "And he's gonna pay for what you done too."

"I don't know who you're talking about."

Junior snorted out a choke of a laugh. "Don't act stupid. I know Boone Pace is chasin' you."

"He's not gonna catch me, though." Mae continued to back around the coffee table. "You know what he did to me." The lie was easy to tell. She'd lie all day to keep Junior away from Boone.

"I know he left you." Junior's eyes made a slow, sloppy pass down her body. "Prolly cause you were bad at fuckin'."

There went using that word ever again.

Mae shrugged as she completed the circle and started backing toward the laundry room door. "Probably."

"Maybe I should try it out. See for myself."

Her feet stopped, freezing in place as the lunch she and Boone shared earlier threatened to add to the mess Junior made of her home.

"That's not gonna fucking happen."

Junior leaned to peer around her. His face split into a wide smile. "Well ain't that just de-vine intervention?"

"I can promise you the good Lord isn't offering you any favors, Junior." Boone walked her way like there wasn't a man pointing a gun at them. "How 'bout you quit while you're ahead?"

"I ain't nowhere near ahead." Junior's eyes narrowed on Boone and the gun that was pointing at her swung to aim right at Boone's chest. "And I ain't quitting till I get what's mine back."

"Camille isn't yours." Mae couldn't help herself. The

need to pull Junior's attention back her way was so strong she couldn't stand it. "She's never coming back to you."

"Like hell she ain't. Without you two fillin' her head with stupid ideas she'll know the way it's gotta be." Junior sucked in through his nose then cleared his throat before spitting whatever he worked up onto her carpet.

She was going to make him pay for that.

For all of this.

For threatening Boone.

For hurting Camille and Calvin.

For setting her restaurant on fire.

Junior leveled the gun back her way. "I knew you was lyin' about him. I should shoot you just for that."

Boone immediately stepped between them. "You're not shooting anyone."

"I think you and me's on two different pages." Junior sneered at Boone. "You Paces think you're so fuckin' special. Think you can just go around doin' whatever you want." Junior's fat finger twitched on the trigger.

She couldn't just let him shoot Boone. He'd made her promises, and damn it she was collecting on them this time, come hell or high water. Her eyes bounced around the space, looking for something, anything that she could use against Junior.

Her eyes landed on the wide cast iron baking tray she used as a centerpiece on her coffee table.

Heavy.

Solid.

Definitely capable of knocking the absolute shit out of someone.

Specifically a wife-beating alcoholic waste of a skin bag.

Boone tipped his head toward the windows a foot behind Junior's back. The blinds were pulled all the way to the tops of the sashes, letting the afternoon light pour into the space she built with her bare hands. "I can tell you right now my brothers are gonna be looking up at the windows in about thirty seconds wonderin' where I am. When they see your fat ass they'll be up here so fast it'll make your head spin."

Junior's sneer widened to a sickening smile. "Four Pace peckers at once." His eyes came Mae's way. "And one bitch."

"You can't shoot us all, Junior. You're not fast enough. One of us is gonna get you, and I can promise when that happens you'll wish you'd saved a bullet for yourself."

"Guess I'll just have to shoot you before they get here then."

Mae didn't have time to breathe.

Didn't get the chance to blink.

The sound of the gunshot was consuming, ringing in her ears as Boone stumbled back.

Junior aimed again.

No fucking way.

Mae took two steps, grabbed the tray with both hands and kept moving, using momentum and rage to propel her forward as she swung as hard as she could, catching Junior right in the center of his ugly face. The sound of the iron against his skull was a dull thud softened by a sickening sort of crunch.

Junior's body tipped back, his weight and the force of her hit sending him straight for the windows she worked so hard to restore.

For the second time, Junior Shepard broke one of her windows.

But this one would definitely be the last.

She didn't watch him topple out. Didn't look to see if he tried to stop his fall from the second-story window.

Because there was only one thing that mattered.

Mae turned to find Boone gripping his left shoulder as blood seeped into the cotton of his t-shirt. "He hit you." Mae rushed at him as the bite of fear finally dug in.

"I'm okay." Boone winced as he worked her under his good arm, keeping pressure on the wound as he managed to pull her close. "Are you okay?"

"No." She pressed her face into his shirt, sucking in air. "He tried to kill you."

"But he didn't." Boone's voice was low and even. "Because you stopped him."

CHAPTER TWENTY-THREE

"WHAT DO YOU think?" Boone stood on one side of the bed dominating the space of the small cabin currently serving as his home.

And now Mae's.

"It seems bigger in here." She eyed the queen-sized mattress. "Bigger than I expected."

"Not sure we would both fit comfortably in a double." He sat on the edge and bounced a little. "Come try it out."

Mae eased down beside him. "It's definitely more comfortable than what you had going on in here before." She barely smiled. "And it will be nice to have a little more privacy."

They'd been at The Inn since Junior tried to burn The Wooden Spoon down, thinking he could take back the control he'd managed to have for way too long.

But Junior failed to realize most women didn't take too kindly to things like that. His ignorance ended up being his undoing.

Mae ran one hand across the blankets he'd wrestled in

place with his one good arm while she was off visiting Camille at The Inn. "This is really pretty." She fingered the bit of white lace edging one of the decorative pillows.

"You have Nora to thank for that. Not me."

Her lips twisted into a truer version of a smile. "Yeah. I figured that out right away." Mae took a deep breath and let it back out again as her expression fell. "This sucks."

"I know." Boone pulled her close with the arm he could lift without pain. "It'll get better every day, though. I promise."

"If Junior just would have left when I told him to—"

"Then he would be trying to figure out another way to punish you for being a good friend." He hated that she felt guilty for knocking that prick out the window. "As it is he's got a long road ahead of him." Boone stroked down the skin of her arm. "And then he gets to go to prison."

"It's just all so stupid." Mae pulled one of the pillows onto her lap. "Junior has a little boy. Why couldn't he just not be a dick?"

"Not everyone worries about being a good parent the way they should. Some people only care about themselves and what's best for them." Boone reached out to slide one hand through Mae's long hair. "Calvin will be okay. Hopefully even better than that."

Mae pursed her lips, moving them from one side to the other. "Your dad's already introducing him as his grandson." She peeked Boone's way. "You should have seen Calvin's face when he said it." She sniffed a little and blinked a few times. "You could tell it meant something to him."

"That little boy will have plenty of men stepping up to show him how a real man treats the people he claims to love." He would be one of them. "You want to take a trip into town and see how things are going at The Wooden Spoon?" He held his breath, worried she might shoot the idea down.

And then he'd be screwed.

Mae held up really well while shit was going down, but once things calmed down she struggled to wrap her mind around everything she'd seen.

The reality of the life Camille lived.

Mae wiped at her nose. "Sure."

He'd tried everything he could think of to help pull her out of the place she'd been stuck in. Flowers. Cards. The new bed.

All the damn ice cream he could get his hands on.

Nothing seemed to help which meant it was time to consider that maybe he wasn't the one who could do it.

"Come on." Boone held one hand out to her. "Let's go check on your baby and I'll take you for ice cream after."

"Okay." Mae let him pull her up from the bed.

Boone loaded her into his truck and headed into town.

Hopefully the surprise he had for her would go a long way into reminding Mae of all she was. What she meant to the town. To her friends.

What she'd built all on her own.

Mae straightened in her seat a little as they turned onto Main Street. "What's going on?"

"Looks like you're not the only one checking on The Wooden Spoon." A crowd of people lined the sidewalk and street in front of the building. Two police cruisers blocked off the street.

Tables lined the blacktop and Mae's favorite ice cream shop dished out sundaes from a portable chiller.

Boone parked his truck as Mae stared out the windshield. "What are they doing?"

"They came for you. To take care of you the way you took care of all of them." Boone turned to her. "You want to go out there?"

A line of women collected just in front of the diner's new front window. Each one smiled in their direction.

Even Camille.

Mae's hand went over her mouth. "The window's in."

Boone tipped his head in a nod. "And the new door went up this morning."

"Oh my gosh." Mae pointed at the handcrafted door one of her employee's husbands busted his ass to get done. "It looks just like the last one."

"I told you everything would be just as good as new, Mae." He reached out to slide one hand down her cheek. "And I intend to make sure that happens."

He'd taken over most of the day-to-day management of the restoration of The Wooden Spoon. Being there was too much for Mae after what happened with Junior.

Hopefully today could be the first step in fixing that.

Clara waved from where she stood with the rest of the women who helped him organize today's little get-together.

"You want to go visit with your friends?"

Mae tried to hide what she was going through from her friends, especially Camille, but they knew her well enough to see she was struggling.

And they wanted to fix it as much as he did.

Nora gave her a beckoning wave with one hand.

Mae opened her door, eyes scanning the crowd as she climbed out of the truck. "I can't believe this."

Carmen, the baker at The Wooden Spoon, stood at the edge of the crowd, her husband Jim at her side. She caught Mae in a tight hug.

Mae smiled at Jim. "The door is beautiful. Thank you."

The rest of her staff moved in around Mae. With every hug and hello he could almost see the weight coming off her shoulders.

Once she reached Liza, Mae's smile was as real as he'd seen in weeks. Liza and the rest of the women pulled her toward the door to the diner, dragging her inside for the first time since the day she knocked Junior out the window.

And saved both their lives. Maybe more.

Boone fell back as the women took her through the mostly-finished dining room. Luckily he knew plenty of guys from the construction of The Inn, and most of them had partaken in Mae's cooking, which meant they were just as eager to get The Wooden Spoon back up and running as she was.

"You got shit done, didn't you?" Brody came to his side, watching as the women found their way to one of the new tables he found to replace the handcrafted ones that were destroyed by the fire.

"It's not perfect, but it's pretty damn close." Ten years ago he'd promised to do whatever it took to make Mae's dreams come true, and now he was finally making good on that promise.

"You know my house gets built first, right?" Brody originally had the construction team set to break ground on the house he was itching to move his family into, but after the fire they'd been able to postpone and take on The Wooden Spoon instead.

"I remember." Boone leaned against the half-wall of the beverage station. "Probably better anyway. Mae might need a little time to decide what she wants."

"She might want to take advantage of Nora while she's still here." Brody eyed the interior decorator where she sat at Camille's side. "She and Clara picked out a houseful of stuff in under two hours."

"That sounds dangerous."

"Not when you're ready to get the show on the road."

"I'm definitely ready for that." Boone watched as Liza, the owner of Cross Creek Ranch and Mae's best friend, passed over a bagged gift.

Mae's arms dropped as she took it, her eyes widening as she lifted it up and down. "This is heavy." She dug into the tissue paper sticking out of the top, dropping it onto the table in front of her.

Her eyes widened as they rolled Liza's way.

Liza pointed at Camille. "It was her idea."

Mae lifted a large black item from the bag.

"Oh hell." Boone started to take a step forward, worried the well-intentioned present might not have the expected response.

Mae stared at it for a second.

Then she started to laugh. It was light and airy and genuine.

Camille wrapped one arm around Mae, pulling her in for a seated side-hug.

Mae's eyes came to his as she turned the wide plane of cast iron his direction. Scrolled letters were painted across the center of it in gold.

Don't fuck with Mae.

"OH MY." NORA'S eyes widened under the bill of the baseball cap perched on top of her head.

"Yeah." Mae stood at the center of what used to be Camille's neatly-kept living room. "That's why we're doing this. She doesn't need to come here."

Nora edged toward the kitchen. "I've never seen anything like this."

"It's hard to believe someone could do something like this to his wife and kid, isn't it?" Mae shook out one of the large black plastic bags they brought to the clean-up. "Makes me want to hit him all over again."

She could handle what Junior did to her home. He'd managed to ruin just about everything she had, but the loss never woke her up at night.

What he'd done to Camille and Calvin did.

"The guys got the kitchen pretty cleared out." Nora tiptoed her way back to Mae's side, carefully stepping through the mess of clothes and toys and anything else Junior could find and destroy. "Do you think Camille will want to come back here?"

"I don't know." Camille wasn't really interested in discussing much of anything that had to do with Junior. She'd sort of closed off to anything that happened before she and Calvin went to live at The Inn. "Either way it's got to be cleaned up."

Nora bent and started filling her own trash bag. "It could actually be a cute little place with some TLC." She pointed one finger of her work glove-covered hand toward the brick fireplace along the living room wall. "It's got some character."

A screech came from the front yard.

Mae and Nora rushed to the open door. Clara continued screaming as she danced away from where Liza stood in the center of the mess spread across what might have once been considered a front yard. Liza held one arm out, a snake dangling from her hand.

"It's dead." Liza grinned as she turned to face Mae. "Musta heard how we handle snakes around here and went ahead and did himself in."

Nora didn't blink as she stared at Liza. "She's holding a snake." Her skin went a little pale. "With her hand."

"It does appear to be dead." Mae turned to go back to clearing out the interior of Camille's house.

"You people are crazy out here." Nora jumped a little as a stack of strewn papers shifted, her eyes scanning the space.

"That's one of the perks to hanging out with us." Mae shot her a smile. "The crazy."

Nora moved a little more carefully as she picked through the pile covering the floor. "I'm not sure I'm cut out for snake handler level crazy."

"Pretty sure snake handling uses live snakes." Mae lifted out a frame from the mess. "I think that's the point of it." She ran one hand over the photo of Calvin. He wore a smile that only reached his lips.

There was a sadness in his eyes that broke her heart.

Nora came to stand beside her. "He's a cute kid."

"Takes after his momma, thank God." Mae worked the broken frame apart, letting the shattered glass drop into her bag before going to set the photo on the mantle of the fireplace.

"Clearly." Nora shoved a pile of pillow fluff into her bag. "Otherwise his face would be flat."

Mae shot her a glare.

Nora cringed. "Too soon?"

"You did him a favor." Liza came in with Clara right at her back. "He got a nose job for free." Liza propped her hands on her hips. "I hate the thought of her coming back to this place. It just feels so sad."

"It doesn't have to feel sad." Nora chewed her lower lip. "I mean, if we wanted to try to spruce it up a little I could help."

"Thought you wanted to get back to your glamorous city life." Liza winked. "Not that I can blame you."

Nora shrugged. "I could stay a little longer. It's not like I have any reason to rush back."

"I don't know that there's any way we could swing that." Camille was digging herself out of the financial hole Junior let them fall into and there was no way she could budget for interior design.

Heck, she might not even be able to budget for the plastic bags required to clean up the mess Junior created.

"Oh. No." Nora shook her head. "It wouldn't be like that." She glanced around at the rest of the women. "I was just thinking I could do it as a friend."

The squeeze in Mae's chest eased for the first time since setting foot inside the house. "You are freaking cool as hell, you know that?"

"I mean." Nora bobbed her head to one side. "I do have really good taste in throw pillows, so."

Clara leaned to squint down at a spot in the corner. "Oh." She backed away, her face scrunched up. "Oh my God."

"Is it another snake?" Liza waded through the mess toward the spot Clara was rushing away from. "You've got to be kidding me." She turned to Mae. "I'm gonna need you to tell me exactly how good it felt to smack Junior in the face with that pan after we're done here."

"What is it?" Mae cringed as she moved closer.

Nora leaned, tipping her chin up as she looked in the same direction. "That's gross."

"What is it?" Mae raised up on her tiptoes trying to get a better look.

"It's people poop." Nora grabbed the snow shovel they brought to help the process along and carefully worked it under the pile of garbage and feces before dropping it into a bag.

Liza lifted her brows as Nora twisted the bag closed. "So you freak out over a snake but grown man shit you can handle?"

Nora lifted one brow, her lips twisting into a smirk. "Honey, I've been dealing with men's shit for a long damn time."

EPILOGUE

"YOU'RE SURE YOU want us to do the food?" Mae stared at Clara like she'd lost her mind.

Clara looked back at Mae the exact same way. "Uh, yeah."

Mae's eyes came his way like she thought he might talk some sense into the bride-to-be.

No chance since he was on Clara's side.

There was no one better than Mae to cater Clara and Brody's wedding.

Mae fell back against the chair as Wyatt set a piece of pie in front of her. "I don't make fancy food, Clara."

"Thank God because I don't want fancy food." Clara smiled at Wyatt as he passed off her piece of dessert.

Boone leaned closer to Mae, wrapping his arm around the back of her chair. "I think she's serious, Sweetheart."

"I am." Clara's eyes went wide. "Unless you don't want to do it. I know you have a lot on your plate right now."

"Right now?" Mae looked to where Brody stood at the counter slicing up the pies. "I thought you weren't getting married until the fall?"

Brody grinned.

He'd been angling to get married sooner rather than later, and it seemed like he might be getting his wish.

Clara's smile tightened. "We were thinking next month instead."

Mae stared at her. "Next month, next month?"

"There isn't another one that I know of." Brody came at Mae with a piece of pie. "We have plenty of time."

"Plenty of time?" Mae looked toward where Maryann sat at the end of the table. "To plan a whole wedding?" She straightened. "Wait." She squinted at Clara. "Why are you getting married so soon?"

"We want to have the wedding outside at The Inn." Clara lifted her shoulders. "And the fall is so unpredictable."

"A wedding at The Inn sounds perfect." Boone was more than happy to hear his brother moved their timeline up.

Meant he could work on doing the same.

Mae rubbed across one side of her brow. "What are you thinking of serving?"

Clara shrugged. "Surprise me."

Mae stared at her friend. "You are about the most laid-back bride I've ever seen."

Clara smiled. "It's kind of hard to explain because it sounds wrong when I say it." She leaned closer to Mae. "I don't really care about the wedding." Her eyes went to where Brody stood at the counter with Wyatt, helping as the little boy took over slicing the pies. "I just want to marry him."

Mae shook her head a little. "That doesn't sound weird at all."

Clara's eyes flicked to Boone before going back to Mae. "I thought you might get it."

"Well." Mae huffed out a breath, "Let me think about what might work well for something like this." She scooped in a bite of pie. "How many people are you expecting?"

Clara shrugged. "I'm thinking just all of us."

"That makes things much easier then." Mae started counting off on her fingers. "Maryann and Bill." Two fingers. "You, Brody and the kids." She added five more. "Me and Boone." She was up to nine. "Camille and Calvin?"

Clara nodded. "For sure." She pointed at Mae. "And Liza."

Boone added fingers to Mae's count as she continued on. "Then Brooks and Brett."

Brooks' head tipped up. "Don't we get to bring dates?"

Maryann eyed him. "Who are you bringing?"

Brooks took a step back. "No one specific."

Mae looked across their collected fingers. "So if Brooks and Brett can find dates that brings us up to sixteen."

"If?" Brooks scoffed. "What do you mean *if*?"

"Haven't seen you bring any ladies around lately." Brett grinned at him from across the room. "So I think the *if* is warranted." Brett turned to Mae. "At least I can admit I will be attending stag."

Boone lowered one finger, taking them down to fifteen.

Clara's smile was wide. "That seems like a perfect number."

———

BOONE LOOKED PAINED as he watched the scene in front of them.

Mae leaned into his side, resting her head gently against the shoulder he was still nursing. "You okay?"

His arm slowly came around her back. He didn't have full mobility back, but every day it seemed better. Boone's blue eyes came to rest on hers as the sound of a chainsaw cut through the air. "I'm better than okay."

"This is the best thing."

"I know." His eyes moved back to where a crew of men was carefully taking down the tree he'd worked so hard to save. "It's still sad."

"But now we can keep it forever."

"I guess that depends on what you have Jim make it into." He barely winced as the first cut went into one of the upper branches.

"He and I have discussed a few ideas." She actually knew exactly what the tree should be made into. "Hopefully these guys are as good as they say they are and we end up with a lot of usable lumber."

"Hopefully." He flinched a little as another branch came down. "You want to stay here and watch?"

"Nah." Mae turned him away from the tree.

She hadn't planned to tell Boone what Jim was going to craft the oak into, but seeing his reaction today made her reconsider. "I would really like to use the wood to make a stool for my prep station at The Wooden Spoon."

A reminder that Boone was her foundation. In ways she used to think were bad.

But now thought of differently.

He smiled a little. "That'll be an awful big stool, Sweetheart."

Mae rolled her eyes his way as they walked to where his truck was parked along the newly-spread gravel access drive. "That's not all I want to make."

"What else then?"

"I think we should hang the spot you carved in our house." Above the fireplace she might already be planning.

"Still a lot of tree left." Boone opened her door and waited as she climbed in.

Mae faced him, knowing what she was about to say was a big step. One she was only just starting to let herself consider. "I think we should make a crib."

Boone stepped closer, leaning his broad body into hers as his eyes skimmed her face. "Only one?"

"Greedy, greedy man."

"It's 'cause I can't get enough of you." He nosed along her neck as she laughed. "Tell me."

He asked all the time.

Like he needed to keep hearing it was real.

And she was happy to give him that. Return the favors of all he'd given her.

Accidentally.

And also on purpose.

Mae leaned back to look at his face. "I love you."

"I love you." Boone pressed a kiss to her lips. "Always have." Another kiss. "Even when you wanted to kill me."

"You probably should have been more careful about that."

"I know that now." He grinned. "I heard you're not to be fucked with."

Mae smiled back. "I heard that rumor too."

Boone tipped one finger under her chin. "Oh Sweetheart, that's not a rumor." He leaned close. "That's a fact."

———

BONUS BIT ONE

THIS WAS WHAT she'd been working so hard for. What she'd spent years planning.

And now it was almost finished.

"You don't look excited." Bill stepped in and put his arm around her shoulders, pulling her close. "What's wrong, Sugar?"

Maryann let out a sigh that only somewhat reduced the upset sitting in her stomach. "I don't know."

"I do." He rested his nose against her temple, the brim of his hat shading both of them from the rays of the setting sun. "You're worryin' about our new girl."

"I think he broke her."

"I think you're underestimatin' what a woman will do for her child." Bill's voice was low and even in her ear.

The calm to her storm.

Just like he'd always been.

"Don't even get me started thinking about Cal." Her throat went tight. "What happened to them breaks my heart."

"That's 'cause you put it out there so fast, Sugar." Bill's rough fingers ran down the skin of her arm in a touch so familiar she couldn't remember a day in her life without it. "You offer it up the second you know someone needs it, and you know that girl needs it."

"She needs more than my heart, Billy." Maryann turned toward the man at her side. "I don't know how to fix it all."

"You can't." He smiled, the dimple that grew deeper every year peeking out at her. "And I know that's hard as hell for you to deal with."

She let out a long sigh as her frustration dug deeper. "I should be able to do *something* to fix it for her."

"You can help, but Camille's gotta do the fixin' herself."

"That's not what I want to hear."

"That's why you married me, Sugar. Because I was the only man willing to tell you what you didn't want to hear."

"That's because you're brave." She smiled a little in spite of it all. It was something Bill could always coax out of her even in the most difficult situations.

And this was a difficult situation.

"I'm not sure if it's bravery or stupidity, but I'm sure as hell glad I have it." He nuzzled her neck. "Otherwise you'd be sittin' in a fancy house in California and I'd be all alone."

"You know damn well you wouldn't be alone, Bill Pace." She skimmed her eyes down the line of her husband's long frame. "You can still turn a head."

"Only one head I ever worried about turnin', Sugar." He looked toward The Inn. "You goin' to check on how your girl's doing?"

"You don't want to come?"

Bill's clear blue eyes slid to a spot just to one side of the large building in front of them. "I think I spotted one of my grandsons tryin' to make friends with the little cat that hangs around here." He eased away from her side. "I'm gonna go see if I can help him."

Maryann watched as Bill walked to where Calvin darted across the newly-laid sod, weaving between the scrappy apple trees that went into the ground less than a month ago. The options for the short growing season had been limited, but there was no way she wasn't planting them.

The Inn smelled like leather and spice as she walked down the open hall of the entry to where the space opened up into a large kitchen and common area.

The cowhide rugs were on the floors after coming in late last week.

Nora had finished the last throw pillows this morning and spread them across the sofas and chairs flanking the huge stone fireplace that would reward visitors who came in the winter.

Hopefully they would come.

Camille was working her way across the huge space with a vacuum, methodically sucking up any speck of dust that might have missed her vacuuming session earlier today. The girl worked from the time she got up to the time she fell into bed at night. At first Maryann thought Camille was worried she wouldn't meet the expectations of the position. But after more than a few conversations about it, it was very clear Camille's issue wasn't Maryann's expectations.

Or even her own.

Camille's eyes jumped her way. She shoved on a smile that didn't look quite right as she switched off the sweeper. "Did you forget something?"

"No." Maryann eased on a smile of her own. "I just came back to see if there was anything else you needed from me before tomorrow."

Their first guests were scheduled to arrive in the morning. Just two couples and one small family so they could ease into it, working out any kinks that might arise.

Tomorrow was something she should be more excited about.

Instead all she could do was worry about Camille.

Camille looked around the room. "I think we have everything ready." She picked up one of the brand new pillows and resituated it.

"Except for the cookies." It was why she was here.

The only excuse she'd been able to come up with.

"I have everything out and ready for tomorrow." Camille's eyes drifted to the counter where, like she said, all the ingredients were lined up along the smooth surface, ready to assemble and bake right before their guests arrived.

"I could come help you." Maryann lifted one shoulder. "If you wanted."

She'd raised boys.

Boys were easy.

You just gave them hell and they gave it back. All out of love, of course.

Girls were much different.

Especially girls like this one.

Camille was clearly hesitant. "You don't have to do that. I can handle it."

Hell's bells. She'd messed all this up yet again. "I know you can handle it, Honey." Maryann widened her smile, hoping to smooth over the miscommunication. She'd been tiptoeing around Camille, trying to keep from coming on too strong, but right now might be a good time for a diluted version of the truth. "I just thought it would be nice if I came down and we did it together."

Camille's parents were gone. Had been for years.

All she had was Calvin, and a woman needed more than her children.

She needed friends.

Family.

Even if that family was found instead of given at birth.

"Oh." Camille's chin dipped a little. "Okay."

"I just—" Maryann wanted to hug her. Pull her in and squeeze all the sadness out of her. "I thought it might settle both our nerves."

Camille's eyes widened. "Are you nervous?"

"Of course." Maryann laughed a little. "This is a big thing. It's normal to be nervous about big things."

Camille was quiet for a minute, her eyes staying on Maryann as she fiddled with the cord of the vacuum.

But then her face softened and she smiled carefully.

It wasn't big.

It wasn't wide.

But it was there.

A first peek at the hope Camille so carefully guarded.

She tipped her head in a little nod. "Okay. That would be nice."

BONUS BIT TWO

"WHAT DO YOU think?" Brody dismounted and went straight to Wyatt's side.

Wyatt squinted out across the bare spot of land from his saddle. "It's nice."

Clara sighed as she slid to the ground, giving Edgar a pat before going to where Brody was making sure Wyatt made it down safely. "It might help if you told him why you were asking."

They'd held back on sharing their plans with any of the kids, Wyatt included. The girls would drive them crazy with questions, and Wyatt was just starting to think of the ranch as his home. Brody was worried it might be hard for him if they told him about the move too soon.

Brody glanced her way, uncertainty still lingering in his eyes.

Clara stepped in and grabbed Wyatt's hand in hers, leading him to the only sign of what was coming. She pointed to the small flags marking the area. "See those?"

Wyatt nodded.

"Those mark where our new house is going to be."

Wyatt stared at them, his eyes moving from one to the next. "We're not going to live with Mimi and Grandpa Bill anymore?"

Brody stepped in at Wyatt's other side. "We need a home of our own, Little Man, and I want you to have a room that's all yours." He crouched down and got level with Wyatt. "So I need you to start thinking about how you want it to look."

Wyatt's eyes lifted her way before going back to Brody. "Will it be close to the girls' room? Sometimes they get scared at night and it will probably be worse in a new house."

Brody rested one hand on Wyatt's shoulder. "That's good thinkin', Buddy." He straightened. "You can pick the rooms, how's that?"

Wyatt's dark gaze went across the scrubby grass covering the spot where their house would soon be. "Okay."

"I was thinkin' we might set up the basement with some video games." It was the one thing Brody was adamant about. He wanted Wyatt to have what Dick took from him and this time he wanted Wyatt to know it was all his.

Wyatt's whole face lit up. "Really?"

"I think it'd be good for you and Cal to have a place to hang out." Brody picked a stray flower growing up through the weeds and clover.

Wyatt smiled wide. "Okay." He beamed up at the man who'd stepped in and offered what he'd never had from a man.

Unconditional love. Affection. Appreciation.

"We'll have to get with Miss Nora and figure all that out

before she leaves." Brody passed the flower to Wyatt and tipped his head toward Clara.

Wyatt immediately turned to her and offered the flower.

She took it and tucked it behind one ear. "Maybe we can sweet talk Miss Nora into staying a little longer."

Brody came to her side and rested one hand across her back. "Last I heard Miss Nora wasn't loving her country living experience."

"That's because Liza picked up a snake." Clara leaned into Brody's side as Wyatt went in search of more flowers, picking them from the grass and collecting them in one hand.

Brody's head tipped her way. "Remind me not to go toe-to-toe with her."

"It was dead." Clara smiled his way. "Not that I would suggest you go up against Liza anyway. She doesn't take crap from anyone."

"Not anymore she doesn't." Brody kept one eye on Wyatt. "You think he's okay with it?"

"I'm not the one who didn't think he would be." She'd been trying to get Brody to tell Wyatt for weeks.

"I just don't want him to think—"

"Wyatt knows this is his home." Clara rested her head against Brody's shoulder. "He knows this is his family."

Brody tipped his head and smiled as Wyatt held up the clump of assorted flowers he'd collected. "I just worry."

"And that's why I love you." Clara leaned her head back so she could see his face. "But you don't need to worry. Wyatt knows how you feel about him."

"I want to adopt him."

Clara blinked at the sharpness of the statement.

It was something she knew was coming. Brody wasn't shy about making it clear Wyatt was his son.

But the conviction in his voice caught her by surprise.

"I don't like him not being mine on paper." Brody's jaw set. "I want him to know without a shadow of a doubt that I'm his dad."

Up until now she'd been struggling to care about the wedding. Mostly because she would marry the man beside her wearing a paper bag in a back alley beside a full dumpster.

And it would be perfect.

But right in this moment she realized maybe the ceremony did matter to someone.

"I think the kids should be a part of the wedding." Clara smiled as Wyatt carefully tucked the bouquet of flowers into the front pocket of his shirt. "I think they should get to say vows to us and we should say vows to them."

Brody pulled her in closer and brushed a kiss across her lips. "I think that's perfect, Darlin'."

She smiled. "Me too."

Brody tipped his head Wyatt's way. "You ready to head in, Little Man?"

Wyatt's head bobbed in a sharp nod. "Yup."

They saddled up and headed back in as the sun crept lower in the sky. Once a week she and Brody took Wyatt out for a ride, just the three of them. It was one more thing Brody insisted on.

Making sure Wyatt always knew he was a priority.

As soon as they were back at the house Wyatt was off Abigail's back and rushing toward the porch. "I'll be right back."

Clara watched through the window as her sweet little boy ran into the kitchen with his fistful of field flowers. Maryann focused all her attention on him as he came in, holding out his gift.

"She's going to come kidnap him." Brody led Elvis and Abigail toward the barn. "Probably every weekend."

Clara watched as Maryann caught Wyatt in a tight hug. "Good."

———

Made in the USA
Columbia, SC
16 October 2024